She was sho
her response to him!

"Leave me alone," she whispered fiercely, shaken by the discovery that he was a force stronger than herself.

"It's too late for that," Zack said, catching hold of her wrist and tilting her chin up, forcing her to meet his gaze. "You're proud and provocative and passionate, and I want you, Eve."

"Then brace yourself for disappointment," she said, her eyes blazing, as she pulled away as though his touch burned her, "because I'm already beyond your reach."

He studied her for a long moment before saying, "Some night, after I've made love to you and you're lying in my arms, I'll tease you about that statement." He sounded amused, but for all that, his words were a definite statement of intent.

Jenny Arden, a British writer, combines a career as a college lecturer in business studies with the writing she has always wanted to do. Her favorite place for relaxation is North Wales, but travel fascinates her— both the places she has visited and the places she dreams about for future journeying. In her spare time she enjoys sculpting historical figures in clay and cooking for company. Huckleberry, her Burmese Blue cat, is her companion while writing. He usually sits in a chair beside the typewriter, but occasionally, in a fit of jealousy, will bid for her attention by sitting on the keys!

Some Enchanted Evening

Jenny Arden

Harlequin Books

TORONTO • NEW YORK • LONDON
AMSTERDAM • PARIS • SYDNEY • HAMBURG
STOCKHOLM • ATHENS • TOKYO • MILAN

Original hardcover edition published in 1988
by Mills & Boon Limited

ISBN 0-373-02995-0

Harlequin Romance first edition August 1989

For John

CHAPTER ONE

THE music that carried from the house had an indolent
sound in the summer dusk. The coloured lights that
edged the long lawn and the river-front glowed jewel-
bright and made brilliant fragments of light shiver across
the blackness of the water. On the far bank the darkened
fields rose gently away, while down-river were the lights
of the bridge at Marlow.

Martini in hand, Eve strolled down the gentle incline
to the water. A rowing-boat was moored by the river-
washed steps. There was the faintest slap of water against
wood. She hadn't particularly wanted to come to the
party alone, but Deborah had been a friend since
schooldays, and it would have been mean to have refused the invitation to her engagement party just because Greg was in New York on business and couldn't
be with her.

A troubled look came into Eve's green eyes as she
thought of Greg. She wished he were with her, but when
he came back he would expect an answer from her. After
tonight she had only one day left to make up her mind,
and she still didn't know whether she intended telling
him that, yes, she'd marry him.

In a moment or two she'd have to go back to the
laughter and the talk, but she was going to allow herself
a few more minutes' indulgence to enjoy the solitary
beauty of the Thames at twilight. She sat down on the
top step that led down into the water, resting her elbows
on her knees and cupping her chin thoughtfully. Her

long, dark brown hair fell forward over her bare shoulders.

Here, in the dimness, the auburn streaks were scarcely visible and, in the waning light, and enhanced by the emerald-green, mid-calf length dress she was wearing, she had an almost elfin quality. She was slim and graceful, her body supple and high-breasted, her legs long and her feet narrow in the silver sandals. The shadows caressed her pale shoulders and emphasised the pensive lines of her face. Her eyes had a dancing brilliance, and her mouth was sensitive but firm.

An unfamiliar male voice, resonant and tinged with amusement, startled her from out of the stillness.

'Just thinking, or planning your escape?'

She glanced up, feeling a little ridiculous and unaccountably on the defensive. The fact that she was perched on the steps, and that the man who'd startled her looked a good deal taller than his lean six foot one in his immaculate dinner-jacket, increased her feeling of being at a disadvantage. But his eyes, arrestingly blue in his rather gaunt face, were steady and amused and somehow compelling, making her first hostility fade. Perhaps it had something to do with the fact that it was twilight and that they were together, at a distance from the revelry of the party atmosphere, but she was conscious of a flicker of immediate rapport with him that made her laugh and admit, 'A bit of both, if I'm honest.'

He came and sat down beside her in companionable silence, obviously unconcerned about the treatment he was giving his elegantly tailored suit. He gazed across the expanse of river that for a moment was the colour of pewter in the purple twilight.

Eve glanced at him, noting the play of shadows on his face, the strong planes of his cheek and forehead, the hawkish lines of his brow. His skin was stretched tight over the bone, and the artist's compulsion stirred in her to transfer the strong lines of his face to paper, to sketch in charcoal the profile that was intent and autocratic, like a pagan head on an ancient coin. The evening was warm, so that didn't account for the strange little shudder that ran down her spine.

'Are you cold?' the man asked with an easiness that was as if they'd known each other for a long time, rather than for the space of a few minutes.

'No,' she said softly, the feeling of strangeness intensifying. When this man, with his arrestingly brilliant blue eyes, looked at her, she had the most uncanny sense of clarity and understanding between them. She shook the quixotic notion off and said, 'I suppose we ought to be getting back to the party.'

'So you've abandoned your notion of escaping,' he said with a faintly amused smile.

Her gaze slipped to his mouth, which was firm and mobile and with a hint of humour that meant she had to smile back as she said, 'I can't really escape with a man I know nothing about.'

'That's easily remedied,' he answered. 'I'm Zack Thole.'

'Eve Hallam,' she supplied for him.

His brilliant eyes narrowed a little on her face.

'Hallam,' he repeated. 'Is it just a coincidence, or do you have any connection with Hallam's Boatyard?'

'No,' she laughed, 'it's not a coincidence. I'm Frank Hallam's daughter.'

'But you don't work in the business?'

'I see to the hire-fleet. Dad deals with all the repair work.'

'So that explains why I haven't seen you at the yard,' Zack commented, his eyes travelling over her, not rakingly, but in an assessing gaze that certainly acknowledged the fact that she was a woman and attractive.

The night that a few moments ago had seemed tranquil and serene was becoming charged with the faint stirring of restlessness and anticipation. Zack Thole was a charismatic man, and already Eve could sense a sexual awareness between them, low-key perhaps, but enough to spice their conversation with a pleasant electricity.

With a slight effort she recalled her thoughts to his remark. She thought for a moment of the boats that were in for repair work at the yard, deciding which one belonged to this urbane man who had every hallmark of money and success.

'You must be the owner of *Rebel Lady*.'

'That's right,' he agreed as he got to his feet. He held out a hand to her, making her eyes question his. 'If we're going to make our escape together,' he answered, humour in his voice, 'now's a good time.'

'You're not serious?' she said laughingly.

'Of course I am,' he said, and she thought she detected challenge behind the lightness.

'Well, where are we escaping to?'

'There's a boat to hand. Let's try up-river.'

'It's only a rowing-boat,' she said. 'We won't get very far.'

'And I thought you were a romantic,' he commented, his eyes holding hers.

She was pleasantly conscious of the way her slim hand was captured by his strong grasp. There was something about Zack Thole that had added a spark of exhilaration to the evening.

'What makes you say that?' she asked.

'The picture you made when I found you,' he replied. 'You looked like some river-sprite, staring out over the water. Come on, let's take half an hour or so to get to know each other a little better. I'm not altogether sure that if I let you go now you won't disappear.'

He went ahead of her down the steps, and his firm grasp steadied her as he helped her into the rowing-boat that swayed as she joined him in it. She sat down in the stern, her movements confident and graceful. She was completely at home in a boat, and she was wondering how well he'd handle the oars. Rowing wasn't as easy as it looked, and called for a different kind of skill from that of manoeuvring a luxury cruiser like *Rebel Lady*.

Zack took off his jacket and laid it carelessly on the seat beside him, a glance flashing between them as he did so. A flicker of amusement came into his blue eyes, as though he'd guessed exactly what she was thinking, and a ripple of suppressed mirth went through her as, caught out, she hurriedly averted her gaze. This man seemed to be able to read minds!

He untied the boat, slipped the oars through the rowlocks and then pushed out into the current. Then, rhythmically, he took the oars, feathering them with easy skill before the next strong stroke. His shirt gleamed whitely in the half-light, emphasising the expanse of his chest, and Eve found herself watching the play of muscles across his shoulders before she recollected herself and turned her attention to the passing river-bank where the fields rested in the tranquil summer's twilight.

Under the arch of a hawthorn she could see the indistinct shadows of cows grouped together. In the distance the last afterglow of sunset was slowly fading from the darkening sky. In the silvered stillness came the quiet, measured creak of the oars in the rowlocks and the whisper of the river as the boat headed ineorably upstream. Zack Thole might own a sleek, powerful cruiser, but he knew how to handle a humble rowing-boat, knew, too, not to disturb the fragile enchantment that was present in the quietness.

Eve gave a soft, contented sigh, happy to enjoy the moment, her problems temporarily forgotten.

'It's a beautiful evening,' she said softly at last.

'And you're a beautiful woman.' The tone of Zack's voice, with its resolute sincerity, made it seem far more than just a line. 'Why are you here on your own?'

'My boyfriend's in New York on business.'

'I see.' There was a trace of amused resignation in Zack's voice. 'A shame.' A shame for her that Greg wasn't with her, or a shame for him that she was already committed to a relationship? 'But, like you, I'm here alone, so perhaps we can enjoy the evening together.'

The tone was questioning, and her eyes, drawn to his in the dimness, answered him without her needing to speak. They were both without partners and they both knew where they stood. There was no harm in enjoying each other's company for the duration of the evening. In any case, where Eve was concerned, independence was almost a cause, an emotional necessity. Even if Greg hadn't been in the picture, the man opposite her would have got no more than a promise of one evening together, unless he had a determination of steel.

'So, what were you so deep in thought about when I discovered you?' Zack asked, his voice pitched to carry just the short distance between them, the gloom making her more aware of its timbre and pitch. It was a voice she would recognise again.

Curiously, it didn't cross her mind to resent his assumption that he had a right to know her thoughts. What *had* she been thinking of? she mused. Of Greg mostly, and of the inner restlessness of indecision that made her need to be alone by the river for a while. And then Simon, too, had to have been somewhere in her thoughts, because he surely was the reason why she hesitated when it came to the precipice of marriage?

She knew she could always tell Greg she needed more time before she gave him her answer, but she didn't want to resort to that evasion. It was cowardly and, furthermore, he deserved better than that.

He'd been dating her for just over a year, and in that time, certainly at first, she must have stretched both his patience and his perseverance to the limit. By refusing to fix another date at the end of an evening together, she'd let him see she was not to be easily trapped into a relationship with him. On more than one occasion after a date she'd told him on the phone that, although she liked him, she didn't intend getting involved with him. And even now, when his sheer masculine doggedness had made her stop fighting him every inch in his attempt to tie her to him, and when their names were automatically linked together by their friends, she still gently resisted when he tried to persuade her to sleep with him.

Was it because she was still in love with Simon that she somehow couldn't commit herself to Greg? And yet, how could she love Simon still after the way he had betrayed her? Perhaps it wasn't love but the legacy of mistrust he had left her with that meant that, however hard she tried, she simply couldn't trust a man enough to agree to share her life and herself with him. And yet, she wanted a family and, although at twenty-six there was time enough for that, the years wouldn't wait. Like the river they'd slip by, refusing to wait for her indecision. And then, too, if she wasn't actually in love with Greg, they did share a good relationship and there was no doubt about his feelings for her. They were as certain as her total conviction that she'd never again fall in love. Simon had cured her of that for ever.

'What was I thinking of?' she repeated musingly, letting her hand trail absently in the chill, powerfully flowing water and unaware that a trace of bitterness had come into her voice.

She glanced up and met Zack's brilliant blue eyes that held so much astuteness and knowledge. It struck her how much easier it would be to confess to this man, this stranger, in the betraying twilight, the whole ugly drama she had been involved in five years before, than it would have been to have sobbed out her discovery to her family. Yet she didn't tell Zack. Even after five years the hurt and the bewilderment and the betrayal went too deep.

'Just this and that, I suppose,' she said with a half-smile.

'You're very enigmatic,' Zack said quietly. 'Do you know that?'

She smiled again and shook her head to contradict him. He brought the boat round in a wide circle with practised skill and slackened his strong, rhythmic rowing to a lazier pace as the current started to carry them back downstream.

'I'd like to know more about you, Eve Hallam,' he said, his voice carrying with strange intimacy in the now rapidly gathering darkness. 'You interest me.'

'You already know about me,' she retaliated, a touch of mettlesome defiance in her voice, despite its lightness. 'I work with my father at the boatyard down-river.'

'No, that's just name, rank and serial number,' Zack told her. 'I'm interested in more than that, but something tells me you don't like talking about yourself.'

She considered the statement and then conceded, 'You're right. I don't. I'd rather you told me about you.'

He smiled, and the attractiveness it gave to his gauntly good-looking face in the shadows made her catch her breath. She liked the clean, autocratic lines of his face, the aura of understated authority about him. He was a very charismatic man. It was hard to believe he had come to the party alone.

For an instant she studied him intently, knowing that the darkness hid her sharp curiosity from him. He was, she judged, in his late thirties, with the easy assurance that went with success. There was a certain hardness about him too that was compelling, not just a whiplash power of physique, but a firmness of character that came across even on such short acquaintance.

She noted the crispness of his brown hair that was bleached lighter by the sun. She had the painter's love of texture. It made her want to put her hand up to his forehead and feel its thickness with exploring fingers. She was amused with herself at the notion, and promptly brought the impulse under control.

'OK, what do you want to know?' Zack asked.

'First of all, how did you learn to row so well?' she said with a spark of teasing vivacity.

In the gloom she again caught the flash of his white smile.

'I've been messing about with boats since I was a kid,' he told her. 'I started with an old rowing-boat I learned to scull with. Since then I've progressed to better things.'

'Did you always live near the river?'

'No, but always near water. My grandfather was a pilot at Southampton and kept a small boat at Poole Harbour. I used to supplement my pocket money by sculling out to the yachts, doing errands for anyone who wanted a letter posted or a few groceries bought and didn't want to interrupt their sunbathing to go ashore themselves.'

'An entrepreneur from an early age,' she commented, a slight question in her voice, for he hadn't said enough for her to place him in the business world.

'You've got it,' he agreed, humour in his voice.

The music from the party drifted out over the water, and with a few strong strokes Zack brought the boat to the foot of the steps. He made it fast before shrugging on his dark jacket and stepping ashore with sure-footed dexterity. Then he reached back to take Eve's hand to help her up on to the landing-stage.

Brought suddenly close to him, she was dangerously aware of his dominating height and the mature power of his build. The pagan masculinity of his physique combined with his gentleman's white shirt and dinner-jacket and quite flawless chivalry towards her in a way that was somehow disturbing. There was something exciting about him that she couldn't analyse, a feeling of something latent just out of reach. With her heart beating a shade faster than usual, she quickly withdrew her hand from his clasp.

For the first time since she had met him she found herself hunting rapidly for something to say to him, wanting to break the mood.

'What work are you having done on *Rebel Lady*?' she asked.

For an unnerving instant his eyes probed hers, narrowing into a scrutiny so intense that she had the crazy notion her soul lay bare in front of him. But his voice, when he spoke, was prosaic, and the moment when the night had seemed suddenly full of madness and possibilities passed.

'I'm having extra fendering fitted now she's on the Thames, and the hull's being recoated. I've just bought a place in Marlow with the aim of spending more time on the river.' A familiar note of amusement came into his voice as he went on, 'I've been accused of being a workaholic. I'm trying to break the habit, at least at weekends.'

Eve laughed, and together they strolled back up the sloping lawns to the terrace, the beat of the disco-music getting louder with every step. Back at the party, with the magic of the river weakening, it seemed ridiculous that she could have imagined an instant ago that there was something charmed about the vibrations between them.

Zack was an interesting man with more than his share of sexual magnetism. With the understanding they'd established that they were to be partners for just this one evening, it wasn't surprising that she should feel a little gust of life at being in his company.

The terrace was crowded with couples dancing to the lively music under the coloured lights. The party was still at its full of fun, energetic stage. Later would come the plaintive slow music.

'Would you like to dance?' Zack asked. 'Or would your boyfriend have objections?'

'I'm not his property,' she said playfully, though the truth of the remark was evident.

'Or any man's.' Zack completed the statement for her.

'If you like,' she agreed with a laugh.

'I wonder how he wore down that independence of yours,' Zack commented, his blue gaze on her sure and interested.

'Greg has a firm belief that water wears away stone. I think that's why he's so successful. He doesn't believe in the word "no". He simply thinks he has to be more persuasive. In the world of advertising that seems to be a general philosophy. I hope it helps him land the deal he's working on now in New York.'

Her words fell into a sudden cold silence. Eve sensed that, inexplicably, something had altered between them, but there was no time to try and make sense of it, for Zack asked, the shading of his resolute voice casual and impersonal, 'Which company does your boyfriend work for?'

She supplied the name and he nodded curtly, so that she asked with a mixture of surprise and guardedness, 'Do you know Greg Neville?'

'Our paths *have* crossed. He worked for me at one time.'

And they hadn't liked each other, that much was evident. Zack's dismissive, sardonic tone said it, confirming somehow that the dislike was mutual. She hadn't realised that his well-modulated voice could hold such a cutting edge.

Eve might be independent, but she also had a fierce sense of loyalty. Zack was no longer the fascinating stranger whose personality had held her captive a short while ago on the river. He had put a barrier between them, the barrier of letting her glimpse his opinion of Greg.

Her eyes met his with the silent statement that this was where their innocuous flirtation stopped.

'I enjoyed the river trip,' she said lightly. 'But now, if you'll excuse me, there are some people I must say hello to.'

It was a polite rebuff, but effective. She saw that his mouth had tightened and his face was stern. Even the blue brilliance of his eyes had a glitter of anger. It surprised her, for she'd made it clear from the outset that she wasn't available to be picked up. And Zack most certainly hadn't struck her earlier as the type to be a poor loser.

His hard blue eyes raked her in a cold assessment, making no attempt to conceal that he was making a renewed judgement of her. Before, she'd thought he was attractively forceful. She'd been mistaken, she decided with a flicker of temper. He was arrogant, and for the first time she sensed that beneath the urbanity was a man who could be ruthless, even dangerous under the right circumstances.

Unconsciously her chin went up a little. It was an effort to meet the probe of his blue gaze, because the authority that emanated from him was powerful, but she held his eyes long enough to show she wasn't intimidated before she moved away.

She wove her way between the dancers on the crowded terrace and went through the french windows into the elegantly proportioned drawing-room. Glancing quickly around, she was glad to see a group of Deborah's friends standing chatting and laughing near the marble fireplace. She went over and joined them. Included in their circle, she was slightly piqued with herself for noticing immediately when, a short while later, Zack came in from the terrace.

She refused to allow her eyes to follow him, though she couldn't help hearing the compelling timbre of his voice as he fell into conversation with another cluster of people. Later, when she moved away to speak to Deborah's parents, she noticed that he was in the company of a vivacious blonde who was laughing up at him with softly flirtatious eyes. For no accountable reason, the blonde, with her low-cut black evening dress and coaxing little smile, annoyed Eve intensely.

Zack's satiric gaze interrupted hers for a moment. She tried to put him down with a cool stare, realising her mistake when she saw him draw his brows together quizzically and a look of sharp attentiveness and amusement come into his eyes. Suddenly she felt an alarming sense of intimacy with the man. It was as though they were alone together instead of in a room filled with people, and as if she had dangerously and quite unintentionally issued him with a challenge.

She glanced away quickly and was very glad to be claimed in conversation by Deborah's brother, Clive. The engagement presents had been set out in the dining-room, and after a while she wandered through to take a look at them. Without a partner, she didn't want to stay anywhere within the radius of Zack's magnetic personality, where some prickle of awareness seemed to make her conscious of exactly where he was standing and who he was with.

In the dining-room the long refectory table was covered with the remains of an appetising buffet of salads, cold meats and gateaux, but she didn't feel hungry, although other people were still helping themselves. Instead she moved on to the group of tables opposite to inspect the presents. She was standing looking at them when Deborah joined her.

She was wearing a rust-coloured ruched cocktail dress that suited her dark colouring, and her brown eyes were aglow with happiness. For most of the evening, Stuart, her fiancé, had been at her side, and the glances they exchanged were enough to make even a sceptic believe in love.

'I'm so glad you could come,' Deborah began warmly. 'It must be ages since I've seen you.'

Eve, at a quick estimate, reckoned that it must be at least six months, for, although they had been at school together and were friends of long standing, their paths had separated some time back when she had gone to art school and Deborah to secretarial college.

'Aren't we lucky to have such a beautiful evening for the party?' Deborah continued chattily. 'I only hope I'm as lucky with the weather on my wedding day.'

'I'm sure you will be,' Eve smiled. 'September's usually a lovely month, and we may have an Indian summer.'

'How's your father keeping?' Deborah enquired amiably.

'He's fine, but he works too hard,' Eve replied lightly enough, though in fact she was worried about the way her father seemed to be driving himself of late. 'It will be better when Robin finishes his business course at university. Dad will let my brother take over most of the accounting work, whereas I'm no help on that side.'

They chatted for a while longer and then Deborah observed, a shade archly, 'You seemed to be having a very good time with my boss.'

Eve looked puzzled for an instant as she tried to work out who Deborah meant.

'Zack,' Deborah laughed. 'I saw you with him earlier.'

Around Christmas time Deborah had been lucky enough to land the job of PA to the chairman of a rapidly expanding market research company. Small wonder Zack Thole had such a commanding air of authority and assurance, Eve thought, but it scarcely gave him the right to make judgements about Greg, or about her friendship with him.

'That's the tea-set he's given me,' Deborah chattered on. 'It's beautiful, isn't it?'

'Yes, it's lovely,' Eve agreed genuinely, recognising the china immediately as Crown Derby.

She could guess what it must have cost. A hard man perhaps, Zack Thole, but he clearly had taste and he was generous with his staff.

'I'm surprised he's here without a partner,' Eve commented, and immediately wondered what had prompted her to make such a probing remark.

Deborah dropped her voice to a confidential tone. 'He's a widower. His wife died just over a year ago now, but by all accounts she was quite something, and no one can take her place for him. Not that there aren't plenty of women who'd like to try, one of them being the head of personnel. In fact, I thought Stephanie would probably come with him tonight.'

'What's he like to work for?' Eve asked, annoyed to find she couldn't seem to leave the subject alone.

'He's a tough and dynamic man, something of a workaholic. And he expects high standards from his staff. Apparently he started from nothing, so he's done really well to have built up such a go-ahead company.'

Eve asked, 'How old is he?'

'Thirty-five,' Deborah answered.

Eve had thought he was older than that. Perhaps it had something to do with his rather craggy features. Deborah went on brightly, 'Being his PA is certainly demanding at times, but I wouldn't want to work for anyone else. In fact,' she admitted laughingly, 'if it weren't for Stuart I'd probably be just a little bit in love with him, like every other woman who works with him.'

She broke off with an exclamation of pleased surprise as her fiancé joined them. Putting an arm around Deborah, Stuart handed her a drink.

'I thought you'd like something cool after the way we've danced,' Stuart said, his eyes smiling down at her.

'We've just been talking about you,' Deborah said, nestling against him.

'Saying nice things, I hope,' Stuart joked.

'Saying that if I wasn't in love with you I might be tempted to fall for my boss,' she teased.

'Shameless hussy!' Stuart said, giving her a little hug. 'I can see I'm going to have to keep a stricter eye on you.'

Deborah laughed, and Eve asked how their house-hunting was going. Stuart lived in Reading, and they were looking for a house in the Chiltern villages which would be within easy commuting distance of both their jobs.

For a while the three of them chatted together. Eve had only met Stuart once before, but his relaxed manner made conversation easy. Even so, she guessed he would rather be dancing with Deborah than talking to her, so she tactfully left them with the pretext of getting something from the buffet.

Almost immediately, a rather earnest accountant she'd met earlier and who must have been waiting for the opportunity came up and asked her to dance. The disco-beat was lively, and so far Eve hadn't danced all evening. Besides, she thought mischievously, surely the accountant had to be a better dancer than he was a conversationalist, and she had the feeling she was going to be stuck with him.

They went out on to the terrace to the sound of 'Billie Jean', which was a real favourite of hers. Crowded a little by the other couples, they didn't have much room, but even so it was clear that she was a natural dancer, her movements quick and lithe as she swept a quick smile of enjoyment at her partner. But the record hadn't been playing for more than a minute or so when someone obviously decided it was time for a change of mood, and put on Foreigner's 'Waiting for a Girl Like You'.

Her partner was quick to use the change of tempo to draw her close to him. With faint, amused exasperation she rested her hands lightly on his shoulders, refusing to allow him a more romantic embrace as she moved with him to the plaintive music.

When Zack cut in on them it was done so smoothly she didn't have the chance to protest. He put a firm hand on the accountant's shoulder.

'I'm afraid "Waiting for a Girl Like You" is my dance,' he said with resolute, implacable finality as he captured Eve with a deceptively gentle but quite adamant hold, giving her no chance to escape.

'Now *that* is what I call cheek,' she hissed tersely, her anger heightened unreasonably by her awareness of his strong frame and the live warmth of his hands on her bare back.

'It's what *I* call enterprise,' he countered, amused, drawing her still closer so that she was conscious of the entire lean length of his male body.

'I like to choose my partners,' she ground out fiercely. 'Now let me go.'

'Do you know how green your eyes go when you get angry?' he queried mockingly.

'I only know I detest cheap lines!' she retorted in a furious undertone. 'Now, let go of me.'

'Are you going to make a scene in front of everyone?' Zack taunted. 'I don't think so. You're not the type.'

Her eyes warred with his for a stormy instant before finally she conceded with infinitely cold hostility, 'All right. You win.'

'I try to make a habit of it.'

'*Do* you?' she asked frostily with all the more animosity because, despite her defiance, she had the unfamiliar feeling she was in a situation she couldn't control.

'Don't fight me, Eve,' Zack said softly, his voice drifting to an intimate key that emphasised how compelling it was. 'I preferred things between us the way they were before.'

A hot little shudder, intensely sensual and alarmingly pleasant, seemed to go through her at his words. She felt a moment's panic as the insinuating music and soft coloured lights started to conspire against her, making her want to relax into Zack's embrace, to move with him as if they were one.

Already she was more pliant in his arms. His hands on her slim back seemed to caress her, drugging her into compliance, her heart racing a little at the perfection with which he had brought her body into an intimately close fit against his.

The slow rhythm of the music enfolded them. Without meaning to, Eve turned her cheek against his shoulder, her fingers tracing the fine-textured weave of his jacket as she slid her hands around his neck. On one Martini she wasn't the least bit drunk, and yet she might have been, the way the other couples dancing on the terrace seemed to have receded like the shadowy reflections in the river, leaving just her and Zack drawn together in a strange enchantment of their own.

She wasn't sure how long she gave into its seductive spell before, with a slight jolt, she realised how much she was abandoning herself to him. Defiantly she raised her head and brought her hands down to his shoulders to establish a little distance between them. As she did so, her gaze was caught by his intense blue eyes. A glance swept between them, and she knew with a sudden instinctive comprehension that it would be infinitely safer if they didn't communicate too closely. Zack Thole was a very compelling man, but she was practically engaged, and furthermore to a man he had little regard for.

'I could dance with you for ever,' Zack said quietly, his hand gently stroking her back, as though he was voicing a truth she already knew.

'I'm for tonight only,' she breathed, fighting the terrible temptation to answer attraction with attraction. 'And, like Cinderella, I have to be going.'

'It's not quite midnight,' Zack told her.

She slipped out of his arms. It was infinitely easier to re-establish her independence when she wasn't held close against his strong, hard-muscled body that was so much taller and more powerful than her own slight form, and when the music was no longer seducing her into a harmony of movement with him.

'No,' she agreed, relieved to find that both her voice and her emotions seemed to be more stable and reliable now that they had stopped dancing. 'But it will be by the time I've said my goodbyes.'

'How are you getting home?' Zack asked.

'I've got my car,' she told him, her eyes as she looked up at him denying everything her pliancy had promised against her will while they had danced. 'I thought you'd noticed,' she added flippantly. 'I'm the independent type.'

'Yes, I'd noticed,' he agreed, his gaze holding hers for what seemed a long moment, before finally he allowed her to alter the mood between them by saying, his resolute voice amused, 'You're an independent escapologist. And, that being so, I'll see you to your car.'

'That's kind of you, but there's no need.'

'You're not frightened, by any chance, are you, of being alone with me?' he mocked.

She coloured angrily. 'You have a very inflated ego,' she told him sharply.

'And you have quite a temper,' he fired back, unperturbed, his eyes mocking her.

She swept him a hostile look, knowing that they'd established none the less that he *would* see her to her car. He joined her as soon as she'd collected her silk stole and had made her goodbyes to Deborah and Stuart.

They walked along the quiet, tree-lined avenue to where Eve's black Maestro MG was parked, a short distance away. The party had been a large one, and by the time she'd arrived the kerb near the house had been completely taken up with parked cars. She hadn't wanted Zack to escort her to her car, so she didn't feel under any obligation to make conversation with him, particularly when he disturbed her so.

She found her keys and was about to say an impersonal goodnight to him when she noticed with sudden dismay that a brand new Rover had parked tightly behind her, blocking in her Maestro that she'd left fairly close to the car in front anyway. She was going to have the utmost difficulty in edging out. She didn't want to put up an inept performance at manoeuvring in front of Zack, and neither did she want the fuss of going back to the party to try and find out who the owner of the Rover was.

'Which car is yours?' Zack asked.

'The Maestro,' she answered.

'You're fairly boxed in.'

'It's all right. I can manage,' she informed him coolly.

She got into the driving seat, started the engine confidently and then realised she was being rather pointlessly defiant. All she was doing was risking scratching her car and the two that hemmed her in.

Zack obligingly opened the door for her as she switched off the ignition.

'I'll get her out for you,' he offered, his voice goadingly casual and his blue eyes amused.

Normally Eve liked a man with a keen sense of humour, but not when the prime object of his mirth seemed to be her. Coolly she handed him her keys. Zack smiled at her, a quick, knowing smile that was all the more infuriating for being so devastatingly attractive.

He swung easily into the driving seat. He had to shunt the Maestro forward and back a good few times, but he got her car out with a skill she grudgingly had to admire. He left the engine running and she paused, a hand on the door-frame, to thank him.

For an instant she was heart-catchingly conscious of his nearness and of his dominating advantage over her in height.

She hoped she sounded more composed than she felt as she said, 'Goodbye, Zack.'

'Goodnight, Eve,' he said softly, his eyes holding hers captive. 'It's been a memorable evening.'

She knew she should move away, break the sudden spell of the moment, but instead she stayed still as he bent his head to brush her cheek very gently with his lips. It was nothing more than a token acknowledgement of the time they had spent in each other's company, yet she caught her breath as though some tangible current had flickered along every nerve, setting her heart racing.

Till this moment she'd never believed in sexual chemistry, but suddenly her heart was pounding with heavy beats, making a melting weakness betray her to complete helplessness. As if Zack sensed it, he cupped her face with his hand, his graceful fingers caressing her skin as, for a moment suspended in time, his eyes searched hers. She looked up into their dazzling intensity, unable to make even a sound of protest as his gaze shifted to her lips.

She shivered, putting a hand to his shoulder, not to repulse him but to steady herself as their mouths met in a light, inevitable kiss. The heady pleasure of the tantalising sweet kisses they exchanged made her tremble. And then, as though there was neither time nor place, Zack swept her into his arms, engulfing her in his embrace.

She made a soft, bewildered sound as he held her against him with blood-rushing intimacy, his lips parting hers as he explored her mouth with a wild, fierce hunger that sent her thoughts spinning into complete confusion. In a moment's feverish madness her fingers entangled in the crisp hair at the nape of his neck before a shocked realisation of what she was doing made her push against his shoulders.

He released her almost immediately, and she was glad of the car at her back for support, because she felt almost too weak to stand. Her fingers went to her lips as she stared at him, dazed by the mindless, sensuous hunger he had aroused in her.

'Eve...' Zack's voice was low and hoarse, his breathing as quickened as her own.

'No,' she whispered, her eyes shocked. And then, as he caught hold of her arm, she pulled free with the desperation of fright and said on a rising note, 'No!'

She ducked into the car, slamming the door behind her, conscious that her whole body was shaking. With an automatic glance in the wing-mirror, she pulled away with a roar of acceleration, somehow not daring even as she came to the end of the road to check if Zack was still standing, watching her. She pushed her hair away from her face with unsteady fingers, and then pressed the back of her hand angrily to her mouth to erase the sensuous tenderness it recorded from Zack's lips.

My God, what had come over her? She'd gone to the party with her mind full of questions about her feelings for Greg. Now they were forgotten in her dazed speculation about her shattering reaction to a charismatic stranger.

CHAPTER TWO

THE drive to her home in Cookham didn't take Eve long, for the roads were empty. She switched on the car stereo, still more than a little shocked that she had allowed a man she had only just met to kiss her with such soul-ravishing intimacy. But her heartbeat was steadying, and already she was starting to put what had happened behind her, as some temporary madness that had never happened to her before and never would again.

She turned into the quiet road that led down to the river and swung her car into the wide gravel drive of the double-fronted Edwardian house. She had lived there since childhood, moving away for a few years when she'd shared a flat with a fellow student while she'd been studying at art school. After that she'd worked abroad for a time with a holiday company that had fleets of hire-boats in both France and Holland. It had been good training for coming into the family business, and at that stage she'd felt she never wanted to pick up a paintbrush again.

It was after her mother's death that she had moved back home to keep house for her father. He'd been so devastated initially in his bereavement, so completely lost without his wife's company. Eve knew that if she hadn't been there in that first year to look after him he'd have spent all of his time at the yard, eating too little but insisting that he was managing perfectly well.

She saw that the hall and study lights were on, which meant that he was still working. Reaching out to the passenger seat, she went to pick up her stole. It wasn't there. With a slight frown she switched on the interior light, thinking that perhaps it had fallen on to the floor or between the seats, but it hadn't.

She must have left it at the party, and yet she was certain she had had it with her when she had strolled out to her car. And then, slight colour coming into her face, she realised how she must have lost it. When Zack had kissed her with such hungry, sensual demand, and she had fled, it must have slipped from her arms without her knowing.

Impatiently she got out of her car. It wasn't losing the stole she was annoyed about. She expected Zack would notice it on the ground after she had driven off and would hand it to Deborah for safe keeping for her. It was the reminder of how recklessly she had behaved tonight.

She let herself in and was immediately greeted by a little feline cry as her Burmese cat came towards her across the wide hall on elegant paws. Mizpah had been a present from her brother two years ago and, like many of the breed, was a one-person cat. She treated Robin and Eve's father with haughty indifference but lavished affection on Eve. Purring loudly, Mizpah rubbed around her ankles and Eve picked her up as she walked through into the study.

'Hi, Dad, I'm home,' she began.

Her father was sitting at his large mahogany desk, the table-lamp lit beside him and the ledger books open in front of him. Even in the kind yellow light his face looked drawn, and, despite the smile he gave her, his voice sounded tired.

'Hello, Eve. Did you have a nice time at the party?'

Mizpah was struggling to be put down, and Eve stooped to drop the little cat on her feet before saying, 'Yes, it was a lovely party. I've never seen Deborah looking so happy. But I didn't expect you to be up when I got back. What are you working on, Dad?'

Frank rubbed a weary hand across his lined forehead.

'I've just been looking through the accounts,' he said, shutting the book that lay open in front of him.

'We're not running into problems, are we?' she asked, coming to perch on the arm of the heavy chesterfield near his desk. 'We've got a very good season's bookings this year with the hire-fleet, and there seems to be plenty of repair work.'

'There's nothing for you to worry about,' Frank assured her. 'Investing in new equipment just means the cash flow's a bit tight at the moment, that's all. Those two new cruisers cost a thousand pounds a foot to build. It's bound to take a while to recoup that.'

'I don't like to see you working so hard,' Eve said.

'A bit of hard work never hurt anyone,' her father said, his eyes teasing her affectionately.

'Well, don't stay up much longer,' she urged. 'It's late.'

Outside there was the sound of a powerful car turning into the drive and then the crunch of a man's firm tread on the gravel.

'Now, who can that be at this time?' Frank remarked.

Going to the window, Eve drew the curtain aside a crack. She'd guessed even before she saw Zack's tall figure silhouetted in the light of the porch. In his hand he carried her silver-threaded stole. It looked very fragile and gossamerlike in his strong, tanned fingers.

'It's a friend of Deborah's,' she announced with convincing calm. 'I forgot my stole. He's brought it round for me.'

She went to open the door to Zack, conscious that she felt uncomfortable about meeting him again with the memory of how he had kissed her so recent in her mind. She paused for an instant, tucking a silken strand of her dark hair behind her ear. She wanted to be certain that she could greet Zack coolly and with a slight distance in her manner before she opened the door to him.

Yet the moment she was confronted with him she found herself wishing he wasn't quite so tall and arrestingly male. He made her feel altogether too fragile and feminine and, although she met his blue eyes squarely, she could feel herself colouring.

'Cinderella left a glass slipper behind her,' he began, a lazy quality to his voice. 'You forgot your shawl.'

She feigned surprise.

'Did I? I hadn't realised I'd left it behind,' she said. 'It was kind of you to bring it round.'

'You didn't leave it behind,' he told her, his blue eyes sardonically mocking as he handed the stole to her. 'You dropped it when I kissed you.'

She couldn't immediately think of a cool rejoinder. The fact that she could feel herself blushing hotly wasn't a help when it came to a quick reply. She was about to give him a chilly little dismissal of gratitude when there was a heavy crash from the study. She wheeled round in alarm.

'Dad?' she called.

There was no answer. She swept Zack a frightened glance before calling to her father again as she raced into the study.

Frank was clutching his desk, his body bowed. The table-lamp and one of the ledgers lay on the floor, knocked over when he had grabbed out for support. As she hurried to him he sagged and would have fallen heavily had Zack not moved so quickly. Taking Frank's weight, he got him on to the chesterfield without apparent difficulty. Her father lay there inert, his head thrown back, his breathing quick and shallow. Eyes wide with alarm, Eve flew to his side while Zack leaned over him, swiftly loosened his tie and unbuttoned his shirt collar. Frank gave a faint groan and stirred a little.

'Dad,' Eve began urgently, gripping hold of his hand. 'Dad, are you all right?'

Her father's eyes flickered open and he whispered weakly, 'I must have fainted. I came over dizzy as I stood up.'

'I'll phone the doctor,' she said quickly.

'No,' Frank protested firmly. 'There's no need. I'm all right, Eve.'

Her eyes met Zack's above her father's head and he nodded, overriding Frank's statement that there was no need to call a doctor. She went quickly into the hall and dialled the number. Dr Osborne was an old family friend, and she knew he wouldn't mind being called out so late, even if it turned out to be nothing serious.

His wife Marion answered, and was kindly reassuring before she passed the phone to her husband. The doctor told Eve he'd be round in fifteen minutes or so.

Eve went back to the study where her father was still lying on the sofa, talking quietly to Zack, his face very grey.

'Eve, I told you I didn't need the doctor,' he remonstrated. 'I'm just a shade over-tired, that's all.'

He went to sit up, but Zack restrained him.

'It would be better if you lay still for a while, Mr Hallam,' he said easily. 'After all, that is the best cure for tiredness.'

'Well, I suppose I can't argue with the two of you,' Frank said with worrying acquiescence before adding, 'Eve, offer Mr Thole a drink, will you?'

The doctor arrived and Eve showed him into the study, and then she and Zack withdrew to the drawing-room.

'You don't think it's his heart, do you?' she asked anxiously as she paced into the centre of the room. 'He's been working too hard just lately,' she went on, her voice cramped with concern. 'I told him so, but he wouldn't listen.'

Zack, who'd sat down on the sofa, set his glass of whisky aside and reached out a hand to draw her towards him.

'If your father's been overworking, then it's probably nothing serious,' he told her as she joined him on the sofa.

She nodded, steadied by his words. His hand that had captured hers was firm and strong, and without thinking she put her other hand over his hard knuckles, deriving reassurance from his grasp. There was something warm and vital about his touch. Worried about her father as she was, it wasn't a moment to deceive herself with pretence. She knew now why she had let Zack kiss her so intimately. It was because when her defences were down there was a magnetism about him she seemed unable to fight.

Hurriedly she stood up and moved away. Zack made conversation with her, she suspected as an antidote to the tension she was under. She answered his questions about the boatyard and her work, breaking off abruptly as Dr Osborne joined them.

'How is he?' she asked swiftly.

'I don't think there's anything to be alarmed about. He tells me it's the first turn he's had like this, and his blood-pressure's quite normal. But I'd like to be on the safe side. I want him to have some tests on his heart. I'll make arrangements for him to see a cardiologist. In the meantime he ought to have a couple of days' complete rest.' Dr Osborne smiled. 'Make sure he sticks to it, Eve. Your father's a very strong-minded man.'

'I will,' she promised, relieved by his diagnosis and yet wishing he could have assured her that there was absolutely no question of heart-trouble.

Dr Osborne had a reputation for being very thorough, but the fact that tests were going to be arranged left her with a faint niggle of anxiety.

'I'll help your father up to bed and then I'll be going,' he went on.

'I'll give you a hand, Doctor,' Zack offered easily.

She followed the two men into the study and immediately went to her father, taking his hand a moment as she said, relief and affection in her voice, 'Dr Osborne tells me you've been prescribed rest.'

'I told you I was fine,' Frank said, patting her hand, but just the same he was grateful for Zack's firm arm to help him up from the chesterfield.

Dr Osborne took his other arm and together they made their way to the foot of the stairs. Eve was glad Zack was there, for Dr Osborne wasn't robustly built and she noticed how heavily her father leaned against Zack as he started to climb the staircase.

Left alone in the study, she picked up the overturned table-lamp. Some loose pages had fallen out of the ledger. Although the accounts figures meant nothing to her, she looked at them with a slight frown of concentration. Were they the reason why her father had seemed so strained of late? She knew they were running quite a sizeable overdraft at the bank to cover the new investment at the yard. For the first time she wondered if her father was having problems with the repayments.

She was standing with the ledger still open on the desk in front of her when she heard Zack and Dr Osborne come downstairs. The doctor paused in the study doorway to say goodnight to her.

'I've given your father something to help him sleep,' he began. 'Don't hesitate to phone me if you're worried, but I'll look in anyway on Monday.'

Eve thanked him and started towards him.

'No, don't bother to show me out,' he said amiably. 'I know my own way.'

He turned and said goodnight to Zack before crossing the hall. She heard the front door click.

'Would you like me to get you a drink?' Zack asked, advancing into the room, his astute glance taking in how pale she was. 'You look pretty shaken.'

'No, I'm fine,' she insisted, a mite edgy about being virtually alone in the house with him, and wishing he had left with the doctor.

Was it him she was afraid of, or herself? She didn't get time to come up with an answer, for he said quietly, 'I want to see you again, Eve.'

She shook her head.

'No, Zack,' she said, striving for emphasis. 'I can't. It wouldn't be right.'

'Because of your boyfriend?' he queried.

'Yes,' she agreed.

'I don't know how long you've been going out with Greg, but he's not your type.'

'Oh, really?' she said chillingly.

'Yes, really,' he fired back. 'Greg Neville's a superficial status-seeker.'

'I'm not interested in your subjective opinion of my boyfriend,' she flared.

'Then let's switch to something objective.'

'And what's that?' she asked derisively.

Zack didn't answer immediately and the silence was filled with a dangerous turbulence. He came closer, and with every nerve she seemed to sense him coming nearer.

'You don't love him,' he said bluntly, his voice hard.

His statement shattered the pretence of calm between them.

'And *what* makes you suppose that?' she began with a surge of annoyance.

'You want me to *show* you?' he taunted, pulling her into his arms.

She hit out at him wildly, but he caught hold of her wrists, stilling her struggles. Pinioned helplessly against him, she met the blazing blueness of his eyes, her heart clamouring because she knew his intention.

'Don't you dare,' she breathed furiously.

'I find your independence a challenge, Eve,' he whispered harshly. 'Any man would. It's like a challenge thrown down, a challenge I intend to pick up.'

He bent his head, and his face blurred and became indistinct as his mouth tasted hers. A quiver of sensual response went through her as his lips moved gently and softly over hers. She was scarcely aware that his hands were no longer a vice-like grip. Hit by vertigo, she tried desperately to deny the response of her senses.

Zack lifted his mouth from hers and said throatily, 'Nice, but it's better when you kiss me back.'

'No,' she breathed, her eyes blazing as she pushed against him. 'Now, let go of...'

Her words were lost as his mouth came down on hers again, this time parting her lips so he could kiss her deeply. It was impossible to fight him, because the betraying weakness had intensified so much that she was trembling. He arched her body to him, defying her desperate attempt to turn her head away, his mouth exploring hers with a thoroughness that made a drowning pleasure sweep through her. Desire kindled fiercely, flaming unlike anything she had ever known before. Dazed, she scarcely realised she was kissing him back, her body alive with a hungry wanting. It was only when his hands moved lower, holding her more intimately to his taut, sinewy body so that she felt the evidence of his arousal, that, shocked, she began to struggle.

'God, you're intoxicating,' he breathed.

Her legs were slotted between his, the slim course of her body pulled into a tight close fit against his. Fighting to break free from him, she breathed furiously, 'That's enough!'

'No, not nearly enough,' he muttered harshly, kissing her again, his mouth exploring hers with passionate demand, while his strongly muscled arm arched her body backwards to prevent any resistance to the assault of his desire. When finally he released her she felt almost dizzy.

'You were right,' he said raggedly, his eyes burning her. 'You don't belong to Greg.'

The name recalled her instantly from the dark, hot tide of feverish sensation. She'd never slapped a man before, but her hand went up now instinctively to deny what he'd said. Too quick for her, Zack caught hold of her wrist.

'You're a wild little thing, aren't you?' he said tauntingly.

She scarcely took in his remark. She was too shocked by her response to him. In all the times that Greg had kissed her, she had never felt her body start to throb with a pagan pleasure as it had at this man's touch.

She had armed herself against desire and love with cool cynicism, convinced that no man would ever again breach the citadel of her independence. And yet, when Zack had touched her, she'd been completely vulnerable, shaken at the discovery that he was a force stronger than herself.

'Leave me alone,' she whispered fiercely, her voice unsteady.

'It's too late for that,' Zack said, snatching hold of her wrist and tilting her chin up, forcing her to meet his gaze. 'You're proud and provocative and passionate, and I want you, Eve.'

'Then brace yourself for disappointment,' she said, her eyes blazing as she pulled away as though his touch burned her, 'because I'm already beyond your reach.'

He studied her for a long moment before saying, 'Some night, after I've made love to you and you're lying in my arms, I'll tease you about that statement.'

He sounded amused, but, for all that, his words were a statement of intent.

A strange tremor went through her, making her skin feel hot. She couldn't even begin to think of a put-down, she was so angry. Yet her indignation was strangely pleasant, almost sensual and, alarmed by it, she said furiously, *'Get out!'*

'For now,' he answered levelly, before taunting, his eyes alight with devilment, 'Don't see me to the door. I might be tempted to kiss you again.'

'And I'll be *more* than tempted to slap you!' she stormed, stalking out into the hall and flinging the front door wide with angry defiance.

Zack touched her lips lightly with his forefinger as he passed her.

'You can pay for that little piece of provocation later,' he promised as he went out.

Feeling she would explode with temper, she resorted to the only means she had left for displaying her fury and slammed the door behind him. For an instant she leaned against it, hearing his tread on the gravel and then the sound of the Jaguar's engine roaring to life.

Seething with affront, she recalled his intimate words to her, that some night they'd make love, before suddenly, for a wayward instant, she wondered what it would be like to be seduced by a man like Zack Thole. Abruptly she cut the thought short, appalled by her curiosity.

She had no interest in a man who in one evening had proved that, for all his apparent chivalry, he was nothing more than a womaniser. To even suggest she would sleep with him when she hadn't known him five minutes! Still hot with indignation, she marvelled at his audacity. Perhaps no one could take his wife's place for him emotionally, but he clearly wasn't averse to casual physical solace. He wasn't even worth getting angry over, she decided. The sanest thing to do was to forget him.

But making resolutions was one thing, carrying them out another. Even with the anxiety of her father's health, she had to make an effort to stop Zack intruding into her thoughts. It called for a similar effort to get her father to take notice of Dr Osborne's instructions. She had to launch into quite a tirade before Frank finally agreed to take the next week off work and rest.

She was concerned about him, realising how old he'd begun to look of late. He'd assured her there were no problems with the business, but she still wasn't altogether convinced. She'd have liked to have talked it over with Robin, but he was in the middle of his second-year exams at university, and she didn't want to worry him just now.

She drove into the boatyard on Monday and parked her car by the boat-shed before walking in the bright sunlight to her office. The huge garage-like doors of the boat-shed were open, showing the tall hull of a cruiser that was in for repairs. To the left of the slipway, which ran down into the river, was the long wooden landing-stage where two of the yard's fleet of twelve cruisers were moored. The rest were out on hire, and would be away till the following Saturday, when they would come in and be kitted out and refuelled for the next bookings.

Jill, one of the yard's employees, was on board one of the two-berth cruisers in jeans and a check shirt, a stack of clean towels and linen under her arm. She gave Eve a cheery wave. Eve waved back and then went into the chandlery and up the narrow stairs to her office above.

Its small window gave an interesting view of the boat-sheds and the rough land beyond, where boats that had been laid up stood propped against oil drums, looking very much larger than they did when in the water. The first thing she noticed was the arrangement of pink carnations and roses that stood beside the electronic typewriter on her desk. Greg, she thought, her spirits lifting with pleasure as she bent her head to smell one of the carnations. He had arrived back from New York on a night flight yesterday, and the first thing he must have done before going into work this morning was to phone Interflora. He had even thought to remember how much she loved pink carnations.

Impulsively she reached out to pick up the phone to thank him, but at that moment Ryan, who worked in the ship chandler's, called up the stairs.

'Eve, there's a Mr Newson here to see your father.'

'OK, I'll be right down,' she replied, deciding she'd ring Greg later.

Mr Newson had dropped by to see how the osmosis treatment was progressing on his cruiser, and Eve strolled over to the repair shed with him so he could inspect the work for himself. From then on, with her father not in the yard, she didn't have a minute to think of anything but the job. May was always a busy month in a season that ran from mid-March to the end of November.

Outside, the sunlight was glancing off the water. If she hadn't been so busy she'd have taken an hour's lunch-break and gone up-river on one of the launches and sketched for a while. As it was, she settled for a sandwich in her office.

She was sorting out an insurance claim on one of the boats that had been damaged through underwater fouling when the telephone rang. Absently she reached out a hand and picked up the receiver, and then she smiled as she heard Greg's vibrant voice.

'Hi,' he began. 'Did you miss me?'

'A little,' she conceded teasingly.

'Only a little?'

He pretended to sound aggrieved, and she laughed before asking, 'How did everything go in New York?'

'Just fine,' he said, satisfaction in his voice. 'I've had a very successful trip and the deal's going ahead.'

'Congratulations, and thanks for the flowers. They're lovely. I'm sitting here looking at them.'

There was a moment's puzzled silence and then Greg asked lightly, 'Is this more of your teasing?'

Comprehension suddenly hit her and Zack came into her mind with blinding clarity. Of course, they were from him! What the hell did he think he was doing, first in sending her flowers, and then in not putting in a card? The blazing conceit of the man, assuming she'd guess immediately they were from him, and, still worse, that she'd be pleased with them! Did he think that all it took was a bunch of flowers and the next time they met he'd coax her willingly into his bed? If so, he'd find he was mistaken. All he'd done was put her in a most awkward situation with Greg. She was about to stammer mis-leadingly but truthfully that a customer at the yard must have sent them, when Greg said smoothly, 'I know I should perhaps have sent you flowers, but I *have* got you a little present. I'll give it to you this evening when we have dinner together.'

Men! she thought. First Zack assuming all it took was a spray of flowers to win her over, and now Greg sup-posing she was resorting to petulant prompting to get what she wanted from him.

'Eve, are you still there?' Greg's voice was loud and called her back from her thoughts.

'Yes,' she answered, conquering her exasperation. 'I'm still here.'

Dropping his voice to a more intimate tone, he asked, 'Did you think about what I asked you in the time I've been away?'

She pressed the point of her biro against the blotter, staring at it with a troubled expression. 'Yes, I thought about it a lot.'

'Do you want to give me your answer tonight over dinner?'

'Greg . . . I . . .' she began.

'Shall I pick you up at eight?' he asked confidently, cutting across her.

'OK, eight o'clock,' she agreed.

'See you then,' Greg said, before whispering as he rang off, 'I love you.'

She put the receiver down and then cupped her chin in her hand as, with an elbow on her desk, she stared thoughtfully out of the window. When Greg had gone to New York she'd been on the brink of accepting his proposal. Now she knew she needed a lot more heart-searching before she could say yes.

Her eyes went to the flowers on her desk and she felt a surge of hot annoyance with Zack, as though he were in some way responsible for her indecision. The idea was too utterly ridiculous to pursue. Surely every woman had a few doubts before she accepted a proposal? It was only natural, after everything in her past, to be hesitant about saying yes to Greg. But one thing was certain: whatever decision she finally came to, she was going to keep the maximum distance possible between her and any man who in the space of one evening could make her react to him so turbulently.

Greg called for her exactly at eight. In all the time they had been seeing each other he had never once kept her waiting, nor had he arrived early. He was a perfectionist. She wondered if it would make him hard to live with, and then, annoyed with herself, decided she was just trying to find fault with him.

They talked easily on the way to the restaurant. He listened sympathetically while she told him that her father wasn't well and that she was worried about him. Seeing Greg's capable hands on the steering wheel and glancing at his dark, saturnine profile, she thought that if she had any sense at all she'd agree to being his wife.

He was suave, amusing company and considerate. She sensed that he was very experienced with women. At thirty-four, divorced and attractive, he had to be, but he never let his annoyance or impatience show when she stopped his caresses from becoming too intimate. He never crowded her or tried to push her. Perhaps that was partly why she hesitated about marrying him. There was never any real spontaneity about anything he ever said or did. How well did they understand one another? she wondered.

Certainly she'd never sensed with him that feeling of completeness that, against all reason, she'd shared with Zack when they'd been alone on the river together. The thought drew her up with a jolt. She had to push Zack out of her mind. He was, she realised, becoming much too constant an intrusion for someone she'd met casually and didn't intend seeing again.

Greg drove them to La Rouelle, a French restaurant that they often went to together. It was in a cobble-stoned little side-street, but despite its unpretentious name and tucked-away location Eve liked it there. The dining-room was long and low, with lots of space between the tables, and the service courteous and unhurried.

They were shown to a table in a small alcove by a window that looked out on to a secluded walled garden. A nosegay of yellow bud carnations added to the summery charm of the place.

Over the meal Greg recounted the details of his trip, his polished wit making her laugh. It turned out that he had to go back to New York in order to co-ordinate the advertising campaign, which would mean he'd be away for a fortnight at the end of June. Greg did most of the talking during the evening, but that was usual.

Quite suddenly Eve found herself remembering again the Thames at dusk and her illusory escape with Zack from the party. He hadn't seemed like a womaniser then. Instead she'd thought him astute, sincere and magnetic. Greg's voice no longer held any part of her attention. The fragrance of the carnations drifted from the slender silver vase with a sultry scent she did not trust herself to smell any longer at close range. That same heady scent had filled her small office all day.

She moved the vase to the window-sill.

'You're not developing hay fever, are you?' Greg joked.

'No. I'm just finding their scent a little heavy,' she said carelessly, determinedly bringing her thoughts back under control.

It was after their coffee had arrived that Greg rested an arm along the table and said with his appealing smile, 'Well, how much longer are you going to keep me in suspense?'

She hesitated an instant before answering, and then, reaching across the table to take his hand, she began, 'I thought I'd be able to make my mind up while you were away, and I think I would have done if Dad hadn't given me that scare on Saturday night. But Greg, this changes things...'

'Changes what?' he asked emphatically.

'It means I don't want us to get engaged at the moment. The doctor isn't certain what's wrong with Dad, but it could be heart-trouble and, if that's so, I'll have to take a lot of the weight of running the business off him. Maybe for as long as until next summer when Robin finishes his course. And I've never felt long engagements are a good idea.'

'I don't see that your job has to stop us getting married,' Greg said, his voice quiet but forceful.

'But if I'm not at home, who's going to look after Dad?' she said reasonably.

Greg let go of her hand and brought his down on the table to emphasise his words.

'Eve you're not telling me you've got to stay at home for ever because of your father, are you?'

'No,' she denied with equal emphasis. 'I'm not.'

'Well, that's something,' he said. He paused as though to make sure his annoyance was in check before smiling wryly. 'I really thought I'd as good as persuaded you. I couldn't bear to have to go back to square one and start all over again with you.'

'Just give me a bit more time,' she said, half in apology, half in appeal.

'As long as I get the answer I want in the end, I don't mind waiting,' he answered. 'We make a good team, you and I, Eve. You're a natural when it comes to entertaining and meeting people. I think we'd go a long way together.'

'Don't make it sound like a business proposition,' she said, though her tone sounded more teasing than it was.

Greg laughed.

'You know I'm crazy about you,' he said capturing her slim hand in his. 'You don't need to hear me say it again, *do* you?'

They didn't linger too long at the restaurant, because Eve was slightly uneasy about her father being alone in the house in case he had another dizzy spell. She asked Greg in for coffee and he gave her the diaphanous silk scarf he'd bought for her at Macy's.

'Do you like it?' he asked as she shook it out to admire it.

'I *love* it,' she said giving him a smile of genuine pleasure. 'It's such a lovely colour.'

'I thought it would go with those beautiful green eyes of yours.'

He drew her close and brushed her temple with his lips before sighing deeply and murmuring, 'I may have only been away a week, but I've really missed you, darling.'

He bent to claim her mouth with his. She slid her arms up round his neck, the moment's unease that she hadn't found the week's separation nearly as hard to endure as he'd seemed to fading as he kissed her thoroughly and expertly. Her eyes flickered shut. She was conscious of a crazy little feeling of relief that Greg could still make her respond to him with the same sweet pliancy. It didn't matter that she'd discovered in his absence that she was capable of a far wilder reaction to man's touch. She was certain it didn't matter...

By Wednesday Eve had received two more sprays of flowers and was getting teasing comments from Jill. If Zack kept this up for the whole week her office was going to look like a florist's shop. She wondered if his sending her the flowers meant she was as much on his mind as he was on hers, and then promptly and furiously denied to herself that he was on her mind at all. She tapped the tip of her pencil impatiently on the desk. She had far too much work to do to be distracted by the memory of Zack Thole's wickedly amused blue eyes, or by the recollection of how it had felt to have his firm lips so relentless and demanding on hers.

Her heartbeat quickened a shade as, against her will, she remembered the look of unconscious provocation she had shot him from across the room the night of Deborah's party. She wanted to forget the silent message of sexual awareness that had flashed between them, yet the flowers on her desk were a tangible reminder of it. Perhaps that was why they unsettled her so much, that and the intuitive comprehension that Zack was sending them with the express intention of getting some kind of rise out of her.

By Friday she was on the brink of contacting him to inform him coolly that she'd appreciate it very much if he'd cancel the order with the florists. As it turned out, she was obliged to contact him anyway. Keeping her father away from the boatyard for four days was an achievement, but by Friday he insisted firmly that he was quite well enough to be back at work. As they had lunch together in one of the local pubs, he said, 'I'd like to ask Mr Thole to dinner one evening next week now that I'm on my feet again. It was lucky he called round that night. Would you give him a ring, Eve, and ask if he'd like to look in? I was thinking next Thursday would be quite a good evening.'

'Dad, do you think it's necessary?' she asked, trying to sound casual rather than extremely reluctant.

'Not necessary, no, but rather a nice gesture of appreciation,' Frank explained, and she realised that the matter was settled.

Back in her office, Eve obtained the number of Zack's company from directory enquiries. It was a matter of total indifference to her whether she saw the man again, she told herself decisively. The important thing was to make it crystal-clear that the invitation to dinner was her father's idea, not hers. Maybe Zack did have every woman he came into contact with falling at his feet, but he needn't think *she* was one of them. In fact, when she thought about it rationally, she supposed it would be quite mollifying to get a chance to demonstrate how very little impact he had made on her the other night.

Reception took her name, and a few seconds later she was put straight through to Zack. His well-pitched, resolute voice somehow overcame the impersonality of the phone, as though even the distance between them couldn't dissipate the magnetism of his character. She found she was gripping the receiver a little more tightly than usual.

'You're one day early,' he began.

The cool, rehearsed invitation she'd been about to launch into vanished from her mind. Completely thrown, she found she was staring at the receiver as if she was staring at the man himself. Pulling herself together, she demanded, 'What do you mean, I'm one day early?'

'I expected you to take the full week before you called me. You're not as stubborn as I thought.'

The hint of drawling amusement in his voice was infuriating. She wasn't used to being laughed at. Somehow their conversation wasn't turning out at all the way she'd planned.

'I suppose,' she said, all the more crushingly because of that, 'you're expecting me to thank you for the flowers you keep sending me. Just how long do you intend continuing this ridiculous practice?'

There was a pause and then Zack said, the quietness of his voice italicising its purpose, 'For as long as it takes.'

She was about to ask scathingly exactly what he meant by that when she realised it would be more expedient not to. Her heart had started to beat rather fast and, determined to deny it, she said crossly, 'This is one of the craziest conversations I've ever had, and anyway, it's not why I called you.'

'Why *did* you call me, Eve?'

It was strange that a man she disliked could make her name sound so beautiful. She cut the wayward thought short.

'I'm calling on my father's behalf,' she said with as much cool formality as she could muster. 'He'd like you to have dinner with him on Thursday. We usually eat at eight.'

'I'll look forward to it.'

He rang off and she was left with a feeling of chagrin and disbelief. She'd been expecting him to start to flirt with her, and she'd been just waiting for the chance to slap him down. And instead he'd just rung off! The man was completely impossible to fathom.

Her eyes fell on the freesias that had arrived that morning, and her puzzlement deepened. Somehow, despite his intimate words to her the first night they'd met, intuition told her that Zack wasn't the sort to find zest in a trivial flirtation with bed as the final goal.

She walked over to the wall-chart to check which boats were scheduled for re-hire the following day. Zack, she decided musingly as she studied the chart, was far more the type to know what he wanted and go after it directly. Games weren't his style.

Suddenly she wheeled round sharply and looked at her flower-filled office as if seeing it for the first time. With a catch of alarm it occurred to her that perhaps she ought to take seriously the thought that what he really wanted with her was a relationship.

Her heart began to pound as though she was in tangible danger. She never wanted to run the risk of a man sweeping her off her feet again. Simon had been her one great love. The price she'd paid for loving him had been hurt and disillusionment. She'd been right to look for a safe, sane relationship the next time in her involvement with a man. And that meant that her future must lie with Greg, and not with the man who seemed set on unsettling her plans and her notions about herself.

CHAPTER THREE

NOT exactly relishing the prospect of having to entertain
Zack, Eve decided it might be easier if she diluted his
demanding company. She suggested to her father that
they might include Dr Osborne and his wife Marion in
the invitation, and was relieved when he immediately
agreed with her idea. She wondered, too, about asking
Greg, but, remembering the dry sarcasm in Zack's voice
that had conveyed such a wealth of meaning in his one
brief remark about her boyfriend, she decided it would
be wiser not to. As he and Greg had evidently crossed
swords in the business world, it would scarcely make for
a relaxed dinner-party atmosphere to have them seated
opposite each other for the evening. And, if a further
reason for not asking Greg was that she didn't feel she
could handle the curious high-voltage vibrancy between
her and Zack with him present, she didn't consciously
admit to it.

In the meantime the flowers kept arriving. When her
father put his head round the door to her office on
Monday morning, he commented with a trace of as-
tringent humour, 'Greg certainly believes in doing things
on a grand scale.'

'Actually it's not Greg,' she told him, the slight colour
that had come into her face at variance with her casual
tone. 'It's Mr Thole.'

Her father absorbed the information and then gave a
comprehending nod, affectionate amusement coming
into his eyes as he studied his daughter. Feeling that some
sort of explanation was necessary, Eve said, almost

argumentatively, 'I don't know why he's sending me flowers. I've made it perfectly clear I'm involved with somebody else.'

Frank judiciously didn't comment. He'd never said anything against Greg, but Eve had the faint suspicion that he wasn't all that enthusiastic about having him as a son-in-law. Not that that would have influenced her in any way had she been sure in her own mind that Greg was right for her.

She wanted a warm, companionable marriage and the chance for children. She and Greg shared a solid-seeming relationship, and she believed him when he said they'd be good together as partners. So surely, eventually, she'd overcome this sense of slight instinctive apprehension at the thought of saying yes to him?

He picked her up early that evening and drove them to the country club he belonged to. It had once been a Victorian gentleman's residence, but had been substantially altered and modernised, to provide among its facilities a restaurant, disco and squash courts. It was set in terraced gardens that sloped down to the river and had an outdoor pool and hard and soft tennis courts.

They had arranged to play a game of doubles with another couple. Wendy and her husband Jason were in their early twenties and Eve liked them, especially Wendy, who, although she was quiet, was very friendly once you got to know her.

The four of them strolled on to the court in the warm evening sunlight. Greg had won the toss and elected to serve first. He was an aggressive player with a powerful serve and a strong forehand, but Jason matched him well and it soon became clear that it would be the women who determined the outcome of the match. Eve and Greg were one game up when it was his turn to serve again.

Eve, standing poised by the net, glanced round to watch him as he bounced the ball a couple of times on the same spot before raising his racket in a powerful arc. His white shorts and Lacosse T-shirt emphasised his muscular build and year-round tan. The ball went hurtling across the net with demonic force. Jason returned it with a shouted, 'Mine!' Greg lobbed it back to Wendy who raced towards the base-line.

'Out!' she called breathlessly as the ball bounced high into the air before she could reach it.

Greg threw out a protesting hand.

'That ball was in as plain as anything,' he stated angrily, as he walked belligerently up to the net.

'It...it bounced outside the line,' Wendy said, a shade timidly, glancing at Jason for support.

'Are you blind or something?' Greg demanded.

'Hey!' Jason interrupted.

'For God's sake!' Greg exploded. 'If we're going to play this game, let's have it fair. That shot was in.' He turned to Eve. 'Wasn't it?'

'I didn't see,' she said truthfully.

He stared at her an instant in complete disbelief, his brows drawn together with annoyance. Then, taking a deep breath, he said with infinite restraint, 'OK then, we'll call it thirty-forty.' Turning his back to the net, he prowled towards the base line. '*Next* time, maybe you could watch the ball,' he said in a sarcastic undertone to Eve.

'And next time, maybe *you* could remember this isn't Wimbledon,' she retaliated.

They finally won the match, six-four, but the altercation at the net had made the mood a little cool as they all shook hands afterwards. Eve, not liking it, suggested that the four of them have a drink together back at the club-house.

'Yes, OK,' Jason agreed as he zipped the cover on to his racket. 'We'll meet you in the bar.'

'Fine,' Greg confirmed with a smile.

With his hand at Eve's back he strolled with her off the court.

'That was a good game,' he said with some satisfaction. 'We ought to do well in the doubles tournament this year.'

Eve glanced back at the other couple, who hadn't yet left the court.

'I wish you hadn't shouted at Wendy like that,' she said. 'Her game just went to pieces after you hollered at her.'

Greg shrugged impatiently.

'She's an insipid little thing. I don't know what Jason sees in her.'

'Don't be so scathing.'

'Well she is insipid,' Greg said dismissively. 'You'd have shouted back at me.'

'Yes, I probably would have done,' she agreed promptly.

Greg smiled broadly and slipped his arm more firmly round her waist.

'I like a woman to have a bit of spirit,' he said. 'It turns me on, and anyway, look, there's no hard feelings or Jason wouldn't have said they'd have a drink with us.'

He nuzzled her ear playfully, making her laugh, and their slight disagreement was forgotten. Back at the clubhouse she showered and changed out of her tennis gear before she and Wendy joined the two men in the bar. Greg bought the drinks. The waitress who served them was wearing a very short circular skirt, and Eve noticed his eyes follow the girl, lingering on her legs as she walked away. It amused rather than annoyed her.

By the time Wendy and Jason stood up to go there was no remnant of tension left.

'How would you like to go to the theatre on Thursday?' Greg asked after they'd gone.

'I can't manage Thursday.'

'Why not?'

'I'm playing hostess for Dad that evening,' she answered. 'We're having some friends round for dinner.'

'Well, thanks for asking me,' Greg said with slight sarcasm. 'Is it my imagination, or have you been colder with me since I came back from New York?'

'Don't be so absurd,' she said. 'As a matter of fact I did think of asking you, but I thought you wouldn't want to come. Dad's entertaining one of the yard's customers. I met him at Deborah's engagement party and he happened to be at the house when Dad collapsed.'

She knew she'd made it all sound more innocuous than it had been and she felt suddenly guilty. Damn Zack, for complicating her life!

'I still don't see why you didn't ask me,' Greg persisted.

'You know you're most welcome to come to dinner any time,' she said. 'What I'm trying to tell you is that Zack Thole is going to be there. When I met him at Deborah's party he happened to say that he knew you, and I very much got the impression that the two of you didn't click.'

For an instant Greg stared at her, and then his eyes became guarded. He glanced away sharply at the bar before picking up his drink. He swallowed some of it and then said with a harsh laugh, 'Well, you're right there. I've *no* desire to meet up with *him* again.' The satiric edge went out of his voice and he went on evenly, 'OK, so Thursday's out. How about Friday, then?'

'What on earth made you and Zack such enemies?' she asked incomprehendingly.

Greg shrugged, for the first time since she'd known him seemingly at a loss for an immediate answer. Then he said, his voice tinged with bitterness, 'We didn't see eye to eye on... a business matter. Not to put too fine a point on it, he fired me over it.'

Understanding the knock it must have been to his pride, she put a quick, sympathetic hand over his. This was a further reason for her to be cool towards Zack. Her ties to Greg made her share his sense of injustice towards his former employer.

'When Dad entertains, I really do have to be there,' she explained. 'You must know I'd much rather be spending the evening with you.'

'We'll make it Friday,' Greg said with a brief smile as he squeezed her hand. 'What would you like to do about dinner tonight? Shall we eat here, or would you like to come back to my place? I promise you I'm not planning any seduction scene with candles and soft music. My intentions are strictly honourable.'

'I believe you,' she laughed. 'OK, let's make it your place.'

It didn't take them long to drive to his house in Chertsey. While he put the steak under the grill, Eve prepared a French salad. The game of tennis had given her a good appetite, yet the meal, although beautifully cooked, wasn't a success. Greg seemed remote and brooding. Normally he was amusing company and very talkative, and their conversation was lively with plenty of banter.

'Greg, what's wrong?' she asked at last.

His eyes came back to her, his brows drawn together in a slight frown of annoyance.

'Nothing's wrong,' he said. 'Why should anything be wrong?'

'I don't know, but it feels as if there is.'

'It's your imagination,' he smiled. 'Come on, let's take our coffee into the living-room. It's almost time for the news.'

He sat on the sofa with an arm around her, his hand caressing her gently in a way that was pleasantly sensual. She rested her head against him as they watched the news together, thinking that if they were married they would share evening after evening like this.

'I can feel your heart beating,' Greg murmured as his hand slipped beneath her loose cotton top and he turned to envelop her in his embrace. For a while she returned his kiss sweetly, her long, dark hair falling like silk across his sleeve as he moulded her against him. It was only when he pressed her down onto the sofa that she sensed he was still angry, and seeking somehow to forget that anger by making love to her. His breathing was harsh as he began to caress her more intimately.

'Greg, stop it,' she gasped.

'Let me,' he persisted huskily. 'I want you.'

'I said no,' she protested, pushing him away and sitting up shakily.

'No?' Greg said, grabbing hold of her wrists and crushing her against him. 'A couple of minutes ago you were leading me on good and proper.'

'What's got into you this evening——?' she demanded, trying to pull away.

'You mean, because I've been so damned tolerant with your Victorian morals up to now?' he said harshly before kissing her savagely.

She couldn't evade him, and his lips were brutal as he forced hers to part for him. Furiously she wrenched herself free.

'What the hell do you think you're doing?' she demanded, half frightened by him.

'How much longer do you expect me to put up with your teasing, Eve?' he said, shaking her.

'I'm not a tease!' she retorted, stumbling to her feet and pushing her hair away from her flushed face.

'I'm getting a little tired of your prudishness,' he said savagely, his face darkened with anger. 'The way you kiss me and then the way you draw back when I start to take things a bit further.'

'A *bit* further!' she flung at him. 'Do you realise you hurt me just now?'

'Maybe you deserved it.'

There was an instant's throbbing silence as her startled eyes met his, and then she said, her voice tight, 'I'd like to go home.'

'Then I may as well take you,' he said with sarcasm, 'because spending the evening with a woman who seems to be frigid isn't much of a kick.'

They drove in silence on the way back. Greg's face was a mask of bad temper. Eve was shaken by the ugly argument they'd just had, and her lips felt bruised by the savage way he had kissed her. He'd always been so urbane and polished before. As he drew up outside her house he said curtly, 'I'll call you.'

'Till you're in a more civilised mood, don't bother,' she said with all the more vehemence because she felt close to tears.

It was the first real row they'd ever had, and she was surprised at how much it had upset her. For some reason Greg had been simmering all evening, and she'd taken the brunt of his anger when it had finally surfaced.

She tried not to let her father see that she was a shade subdued. He was going up to one of the London hospitals the following week for an electro-cardiogram test. Eve was glad the appointment had been arranged so quickly, although since his collapse he hadn't suffered from any further dizzy spells which was reassuring.

Greg didn't phone during the next few days. She felt unsettled and not in the least in a dinner-party mood. Yet she went to the usual trouble with the preparations for the meal, wanting the Osbornes to enjoy themselves. The problem was striking the right balance. She enjoyed cooking, but Zack Thole had made enough erroneous assumptions about her, and she wasn't giving him any cause to think that she was trying to impress him with her culinary talents. Avocado and prawn cocktail, followed by Crown Roast and a choice between fresh fruit salad and profiteroles seemed a suitable menu.

She had just checked that everything was under control in the kitchen and was about to join her father in the drawing-room when the phone rang. She went over to the worktop, untying her apron as she went, and then she smiled as she heard her brother's voice.

'Hello, Robin,' she began warmly. 'How's everything going?'

'Just two more exams to get through,' he answered. 'One in finance and the other in business administration.'

'You're surviving, then,' she laughed as she heard the doorbell and then her father's tread in the hall as he went to answer it.

'Just about,' Robin joked, 'though the revision has been pretty hard going. I don't mind telling you I'm really looking forward to travelling out to Greece the moment term ends. A few weeks' hitch-hiking with a couple of friends is exactly what I need.'

In the hall she could hear Zack's resolute voice in conversation with her father. She was in no hurry to see him, and yet at the same time she couldn't prevent a faint stir of anticipation at the prospect of being in his company again. He disturbed her, and yet there was something dangerously exhilarating about that slight edge of unease.

'Anyway,' Robin continued, 'how are things on the home front?'

She wouldn't lie to him by saying everything was fine, but she did downplay their father's health problem. They chatted for a while longer before the pips went and Robin said hurriedly, 'Look, I'll have to go now. I've run out of money. I'll give you a ring next week when Dad's got the results of the tests. OK?'

She had time to say, 'OK, take care,' before the line went dead.

Without meaning to, she glanced in the mirror as she crossed the hall. She was wearing a drop-waisted dress in turquoise patterned silk with a pleated skirt which made her look boyishly slim, and which she always felt good in. When Zack ran his assessing blue eyes over her, he was going to see that she looked cool and composed and perfectly indifferent to him.

He was standing with his back to her as she went into the drawing-room, admiring a riverscape she had painted of Marlow Weir that hung over the mantelpiece. He turned immediately on hearing her enter, and she said hello politely and with the merest touch of hauteur. She felt she did it rather well. There was no element of unfriendliness in her manner, just the very clear statement that he wouldn't get within kissing distance of her again.

Zack's gaze held hers, his compelling blue eyes glinting for an instant with mockery. Regret stabbed sharply that she hadn't succeeded in slapping his face the other night. It was time he realised she wasn't a diversion laid on entirely for his masculine amusement.

She accepted the glass of sherry her father handed her as Zack said, matching her formality so perfectly she could feel her temper rising, 'I didn't realise you painted.'

'It's a hobby more than anything else,' she answered. 'though I do sell some of my pictures to a gallery in Marlow.'

'I must look out for them. I think I'd recognise your style again. It's very expressive,' he said before asking, 'Did you never think of making a living from it?'

'I went to art school... but...' To her total dismay, though she'd started calmly enough her voice suddenly caught.

Frank put in gently, 'Eve's fiancé was killed in their last year at college together. After that you didn't want to paint for quite a while, did you, love?' The doorbell rang and he announced as he got to his feet, 'That'll be George and Marion.'

He went out of the room, and in the silence Zack said with quiet sympathy, 'I'm sorry, Eve.'

Her throat felt tight. Why ever had she let this arrogant stranger glimpse that she wasn't as detached and invulnerable as she liked to appear? She couldn't understand why her voice had failed her the way it had when she'd been about to mention Simon's death.

She was preparing to move the conversation quickly to a less emotionally demanding topic when inadvertently her gaze met Zack's. Her heart fluttered strangely. She didn't think she'd ever met anyone with eyes that were so vividly and compellingly blue. But this time she didn't like it. The sensation was too unfamiliar, too disturbing and more than a little alarming. What was there about this man that she seemed unable to ward off his masculine charisma?

She was immensely glad that at that moment Mizpah came sneaking round the door and advanced into the room on dainty paws. The little Burmese headed straight for Zack and, seizing on the opportunity to break the mood, she said flippantly, 'You're being very honoured. Usually Mizpah doesn't take to strangers.'

'Like her mistress?' Zack queried with faint mockery.

It pleased her that she was able to come back with an immediate warning rejoinder.

'Cats don't like people trespassing on their personal space,' she said.

Zack, who'd stretched out a friendly hand to Mizpah, glanced at her. She felt the piercing examination of his gaze but declined to meet the challenge of it. Zack smiled faintly and went to stroke Mizpah. As he did so the cat unexpectedly drew back and lashed out at him with a paw.

'Mizpah!' Eve gasped in reproof as the cat dived under an armchair. 'I'm so sorry,' she apologised to Zack. 'She's never done anything like that before. Has she hurt you?'

'No, it's nothing,' he said casually, reaching for a pristine white handkerchief to wipe the scratch with. There was the drawl of lazy mockery in his voice as he went on, 'Placid cats are all very well, but taming the unpredictable ones that scratch a little is somehow more rewarding.'

Eve knew exactly what he meant, and to her annoyance felt herself blush.

'I suppose I'd better put some antiseptic on your hand for you,' she said with a marked increase in coldness as Dr Osborne and his wife came into the room with her father.

Frank made the introductions, and Mizpah's unpredictable behaviour made an immediate topic of laughing conversation about cats and pets in general before Eve went with Zack into the kitchen.

She fetched the tube of antiseptic cream while he leaned against the worktop watching her negligently. She could sense his eyes on her, his masculine scrutiny making her skin prickle. The kitchen was large, yet she had the feeling of being too closely confined with him. His white shirt and well-cut grey suit should have downplayed the animal grace of the man, yet somehow they didn't. She noted his red and mauve silk tie that was artistic and individual. She couldn't analyse why it was that his immaculate appearance made her so devastatingly aware of the rugged virility it should have blunted. Rather briskly, she said, 'You'd better run the scratch under the tap, and then you can put some of this cream on it.'

'I was rather looking forward to your doing the first aid for me. I'm sure you have such gentle hands.'

Eve felt she would choke on his humour. It took the greatest effort of self-will to pretend that his amusement had glanced unnoticed off her.

She went up to him, and then found that, close to, she was far too conscious of his height and build. It didn't help her composure that she couldn't help but remember what it had been like to be kissed with such devastating thoroughness by him. Refusing to allow her eyes to clash with his, she took hold of his wrist so she could inspect the scratch, hoping he didn't notice the slight tremor in her hand as she touched him. His Piaget watch made her more aware of the strong, prominent bones of his wrist. His fingers were deft and agile and, as she knew from experience, sensitive when it came to caressing.

The scratch that ran towards his knuckles was long, but it had only bled a little and she said, finding her voice a little hard to control to achieve the derisive tone she was aiming for, 'It hardly needs first aid.'

'You didn't think I was going to pass up the chance to be alone with you, did you?' he taunted, a hint of buried laughter in his firm voice.

She immediately let go of his wrist. Zack's eyes narrowed on her a little as he studied her. Then he moved to the sink and ran his hand under the tap.

'Why are you so jumpy with me, Eve?' he asked as he reached for the towel.

'That's your imagination,' she told him promptly.

He came towards her and she took a wary step back, the worktop halting any further retreat.

'*Is* it?' he mocked.

'*Yes,*' she said emphatically. 'And now I think we'd better be getting back to the others.'

As she slithered away from where he'd cornered her, he caught hold of her arm.

'No, not yet,' he said. Then, sensing her sharp recoil, he drew his brows together in slight annoyance and demanded, this time without a trace of mockery, '*Are* you frightened of me, Eve?'

'Certainly not!' she denied hotly. 'But I *do* object to being grabbed hold of, and most especially I object to being kissed against my will.'

'I don't grab,' Zack corrected her.

'That depends on how you define the word,' she told him coldly. 'Most men wait for some kind of indication that the woman wouldn't object to being kissed.'

'I'd been given plenty of indications that night I kissed you,' Zack pointed out. 'And all of them were come-ons.'

'Only to a man with an outsized ego,' she retorted, with not as much frosty indignation as she would have liked because she was colouring with the truth of what he'd said. 'And now, let go of me.'

'I will,' he said calmly, 'as soon as you tell me when I can see you again.'

'The answer to that is, you can't.'

His mouth quirked into an amused smile.

'Have dinner with me tomorrow night,' he said.

'Do you know I've just about had it up to here with men who don't understand the meaning of the word "no"?'

'I take it we're talking about the boyfriend.'

She didn't answer and was about to pull away from him and return to the drawing-room when he resisted her attempt and asked, '*Do* I take it you've said "no" to him?'

'That is none of your business.'

His eyes probed hers for an instant with a silent challenge, and with a cool glance she preceded him into the hall, conscious that her heart was racing. The strange thing was that, although she'd had the last word for once, as she heard his lithe footfall close behind her, she knew as clearly as if he'd made the statement aloud that he intended making it his business.

It was all very well for intuition to tell her Zack wasn't playing games with her, but reason told her otherwise. If her sense of intuition had been reliable, Simon could have never deceived her the way he had. It was far wiser to trust reason than intuition, and, looked at coolly and unemotionally, no man after one evening in a woman's company decided she was everything he wanted in a lifetime mate.

Yet, despite her slight reserve with him, the dinner went well. The conversation seemed livelier than usual and Zack, she had to admit, was stimulating company. There was something bracing about him that she couldn't help but respond to, and the meal ended with her being drawn into a joking argument with him, prompted by a recent television serial.

Shortly after ten the Osbornes left, as the doctor had to be at the hospital early the next morning. The talk soon turned to the boatyard and from there to business matters.

Eve went into the kitchen to make more coffee. With quite a bit of tidying up to be done after the meal, it was a little while before she returned to the drawing-room.

As she went in she heard Zack say, 'I'll need to see the last few years' accounts and then to look round the yard itself. After that I'll give you a decision.'

She set the tray she was carrying down on the coffee-table and looked enquiringly at her father.

'Mr Thole's interested in investing in the boatyard,' he explained.

She simply couldn't believe it. It prompted her into saying, almost before she'd thought, 'But, Dad, it's a family business.'

'I suppose it could still stay that way,' Zack countered mockingly, his vivid blue eyes holding hers.

'I'm afraid I fail to see how,' she said coldly, her voice a shade breathless, for it didn't seem possible she could have understood him correctly.

'Then I must spell it out some time,' he replied, his tone perfectly amiable, though she caught the ring of steel behind it.

'The boatyard...'

'Eve,' her father interrupted pleasantly, 'would you pour the coffee?'

He gave her a mute glance of appeal, and with the third jolt in as many minutes she realised how very anxious he was that she should not jeopardise what he and Zack had discussed. Frank shifted the conversation to a lighter topic, and with an effort Eve sustained the appearance of being quietly charming to one of her father's guests.

When finally Zack stood up to leave, Frank left it to her to see him out.

'I'd no idea you could be so obedient,' Zack remarked.

It wasn't worth the pretence of making out she didn't know what he was talking about. Zack was far too astute to have missed the look her father had given her when she'd brought the coffee in.

'You haven't bought into the business yet,' she reminded him pointedly.

'No, but I'm going to, just as you and I are going to end up being lovers.'

'That is the most preposterous and arrogant statement I've ever heard!' she spluttered.

'Are you going to deny the attraction between us? Because it's been there ever since the first moment we met,' he said, forcefulness in his voice as he took hold of her by the forearms and pulled her to his chest.

'Let go of me,' she demanded. 'What happened that night was the effect of twilight and the river. But the enchantment's over now and I'm sane.'

'I think I could get you to act a little wild again without too much difficulty,' he said, his eyes deliberately travelling to her mouth.

'No...' she gasped, hampered more than a little by the fact that her father was in the drawing-room.

Amusement glittered in his eyes as he let her go.

'When I do, I'll pick a better place,' he said, almost as if he read her thoughts. 'Goodnight, Eve.'

He left the house, and she realised furiously that it was too late to point out that she was committed to a relationship, and that, even if she hadn't been, she had no intention of getting involved with anyone as dangerous as he was. Become his bed partner? He'd wait for ever for that! Transient affairs might satisfy him, with his hedonistic outlook, but she wanted something lasting. His gall at even suggesting she could consider becoming his mistress made her blaze with anger.

She stormed back into the drawing-room, where her father was sitting deep in thought.

'Dad, what on earth's going on that you're contemplating that ... man coming into the business with us?' she began.

Frank drew a deep breath and reached for the brandy-glass that was on the coffee-table in front of him.

'That man,' he repeated her words, relief in his voice, 'has come up with a proposition that could be the salvation of the boatyard.'

'Salvation?' she said, aghast, her anger with Zack momentarily forgotten. 'But, Dad, you told me everything was all right with the financial side of the business. Just how bad are things? What have you been keeping from me?'

'We're on a knife's edge, Eve,' her father said wearily. 'I didn't tell you because I didn't want to worry you, but we're at our credit limit with the bank, and my getting ill has been the last straw. With an injection of capital, the boatyard would have the chance to get on its feet again.'

'I don't want Zack in the business,' she said emphatically. 'You know what you've always said, that Robin's to take it over when you retire. The boatyard's always been a family concern, ever since it was started. I don't want an outsider mixed up in it, and I know Robin's going to feel the same way.'

'Without Mr Thole, there may be no business for Robin to come into,' Frank said bluntly, before adding more gently, 'Listen, love, I understand how you feel, and in many ways I feel the same. But Mr Thole won't have anything to do with the day-to-day running of the business and, in any case, I thought you rather liked him.'

'I can't stand him,' she said hotly.

Frank looked at her with mild surprise and then suddenly drew his brows together sharply. He put a hand up to his forehead, making Eve ask in alarm, 'Dad, are you all right?'

'I'm feeling a little dizzy,' he said, his voice confused. 'It'll pass in a minute.'

And, frightened about his health, Eve not only let the subject drop, she made no further protests when he talked over the matter with her again later.

CHAPTER FOUR

IT WAS the following morning when Greg phoned Eve at work.

'Hi,' he began with a little too much casualness. 'I thought I'd give you a ring to check that we're still on for the theatre tonight. I've got tickets for *Forty-Second Street*. Is that OK with you?'

'That's fine with me,' she said, finding it hard to be completely spontaneous with him after their row.

'I'll call for you at seven, then,' he said, before adding after a brief pause, 'Eve...look, I'm sorry about the other night. Put it down to frustration and a bad day at work.'

'It was my fault too,' she said immediately. 'I know I'm not being fair to you, keeping you waiting for an answer.'

'Don't be silly,' Greg said, a smile in his voice. 'Anyway, you're worth waiting for.'

Eve felt better now that she and Greg had made up, and she enjoyed the theatre and the weekend that followed. Yet she couldn't help the worry about her father intruding into her thoughts. She went with him to the hospital on Tuesday and was enormously relieved when the specialist said that Frank showed no sign of heart-trouble.

She and her father were sitting over coffee, relaxed after the strain of waiting for the results of the tests, when Eve said, 'Why don't you go and spend a few days with Aunt Mary? You know how you like Wroxham, and she'd love to have you.'

Now that it seemed that her father's dizzy spells had been caused by overwork, she wanted him to rest until he was really fit again. To her surprise, he didn't resist her suggestion.

'I think you're right, Eve,' he said. 'A few days off work would do me good, and I could have a look round the boatyards there to see what their latest cabin cruisers are like.'

Eve smiled at his inability to accept the idea of a complete rest, and quietly decided to ring her aunt and get her to persuade Frank to extend his holiday to at least a week.

She was with him in his office on Wednesday afternoon, checking the work he wanted her to see to while he was away in Norfolk, when the phone rang. Frank answered it. Eve glanced up as she heard him say hello to Zack and then realised that she was filing the papers she'd gathered up in completely the wrong order. She corrected the mistake, noting from the pleased timbre of her father's voice that the proposed deal with Zack was likely to go ahead.

'Yes,' she heard Frank say, 'of course that can be arranged. When would you like to look round the yard? I'm afraid I shall be away for a couple of days, but...'

'I'll show him round,' Eve whispered immediately, not wanting her father to cancel his holiday.

'... but my daughter will be here and she'll be able to answer any queries you may have,' Frank continued. There was a pause and then he handed the phone to her and said, 'Mr Thole would like a word with you.'

She took hold of the receiver, making the firm mental resolution that her own personal feelings weren't going to jeopardise her father's business negotiations. For some reason, she felt as if she was about to connect with some intangible source of danger. Abandoning the quixotic notion, she began, her voice cool, but amiable, 'Good afternoon, Mr Thole.'

'Good afternoon,' Zack matched her formality before adding with deliberate provocation, 'partner.'

It took the greatest self-control not to retaliate, but five years' experience in the business had taught her never to appear riled, however taxed she might feel with a client.

'When would you like to call in at the yard?' she asked calmly.

'My, aren't you just on your best behaviour today, my little water-sprite!'

At that moment Frank was called out of the office by a customer. Forgetting her resolve, Eve said frostily, 'Listen, Mr Thole, we're not on the river now.'

'And as it so happens I don't believe in getting personal relationships tangled up with business. It complicates life too much. So when I decide to pick up from where the two of us left off that night, I'll let you know.'

For an instant she was speechless with anger at his male presumptuousness. Controlling her temper was like holding a lid down on a boiling saucepan, but somehow she managed it.

'There's nothing to pick up on,' she said very precisely.

'We'll argue about that later,' he said. 'In the meantime, I'll be in touch about looking over the boatyard.'

She heard him ring off. Never once in an exchange of words with him did she come off the winner. She replaced the receiver and glared at the phone as though it, and not Zack, was the object of her affront.

She only hoped her father would be back from Norfolk when Zack called in. That way she need have nothing to do with him, and perhaps when he realised that, despite the way she'd kissed him that first night, he wasn't going to get anywhere with her, he'd stop the ridiculous practice of sending her flowers every day.

Frank left for Wroxham the next day and Eve spent the rest of the week putting in long hours at the boatyard. She had given little time to her painting of late, and she decided that if she cleared up all the outstanding paperwork before the weekend she'd reward herself by devoting Sunday entirely to her art.

She had just arrived home, having finished work at lunch time on Saturday, when she heard the erratic throb of a car engine as it turned into the drive. Recognising it, she ran to the front door to see her lanky brother getting out of the driving seat of his old Fiat. He was wearing faded jeans and a Bristol University T-shirt. He stretched his cramped shoulders and then, seeing her, his face broke into a smile.

'Hi, Eve,' he said, giving her a brotherly hug.

'Robin, I didn't expect you home till some time next week!' she laughed.

'Term's as good as finished now,' he explained. 'There didn't seem much point in sticking around, and I wanted a few days of home before I leave for Greece.'

'Well, it's lovely to see you. Have you had lunch?'

'No, not yet.'

'Neither have I. Let's have a quick cup of coffee, and then why don't we go down to the river and have a pub lunch outside?'

'Great,' Robin agreed, before saying as they went indoors, 'I take it Dad's gone to Wroxham?'

'That's right. Why?'

'Well, I knew you'd be out with Greg this evening so I wanted to time my arrival so we could have that serious chat you mentioned on the phone. Dad's tests at the hospital were OK, so what's so serious?'

'The business,' Eve told him. 'You didn't sound very happy when Dad mentioned to you he was hoping to get an outside investor to put money into the yard.'

'Tell you what,' Robin said, 'I'll cart my gear inside and we'll thrash it out over lunch.'

They were sitting at a wooden table overlooking the Thames, eating cold-meat salads, when Eve brought the conversation back to the financial problems the boatyard was facing. Robin heard her out and then took a sip of lager and leaned an elbow on the table.

'I've had more time to think about this idea of having a silent partner in the business now,' he said. 'At first I didn't like it, but if this Mr Thole is willing to invest, then I'm going to tell Dad I'm in agreement. He took a gamble when he expanded, and ultimately, if we can just weather this bad patch, it's going to pay off. In which case, if we still want to we can buy Mr Thole out.'

Eve smiled. 'I'm glad you're happy with the plan, because I don't think Dad ought to take too much strain from now on.'

'What's Mr Thole like?' Robin asked.

Eve thought for a minute and then said, striving to be impartial, 'As I understand it, he's something of a whizz-kid. I'd say he's very hard-headed when it comes to business, and from what I've seen it looks as if he's got the Midas touch.'

'But you don't like him?' Robin queried astutely.

Eve shrugged lightly and said, 'He's very sure of himself.'

'I'm sure you're more than a match for him,' Robin grinned.

But somehow Eve didn't share his confidence. Put simply, Zack Thole was the most unsettling man she had ever met. She loathed his male arrogance, the way she invariably came off worst in their verbal tilts, the curious magnetism that flared between them which meant that not for one single second when she was with him could she forget that she was a woman. And when she thought of the way he had pulled her into his arms and kissed her, fitting her against his hard body as though she were intimate with him, she burned hot with indignation. At least, she assumed it was indignation, for it was strange how sensual her reaction to the recollection seemed, sensual and disturbing.

She wished she never had to see him again. Even more so, she wished she could forget his prediction that eventually they would become lovers. It both maddened her and made her heartbeat quicken with a faint edge of apprehension. But what made her angriest of all was the intuitive comprehension that if Zack ever did take her, he would make sure she enjoyed it.

She was getting ready to take her small motorboat for a trip on the river on Sunday morning when Zack's Jaguar turned in through the boatyard's entrance. A moment before, she had been enjoying the luxury of the hot June sun on her bare skin. Now she felt suddenly alarmingly vulnerable in her brief green and gold bikini. It was ideal for getting a tan while she sat outside at a table, sketching, but it was the last thing she would have worn if she'd known she was going to encounter Zack, whose blue eyes never seemed to miss the slightest detail of her appearance. She had a matching wrap-around skirt, but she had left it in her office and it was too late to fetch it.

Zack got out of the Jaguar and came towards her with easy animal grace. She hadn't seen him in casual clothes before, and his raw virility made her almost catch her breath. He was wearing an open-necked check shirt and blue jeans that showed lean-muscled thighs which emphasised his pantherlike stride. He looked as hard and as fit as an athlete. In a city suit his attractiveness had been disturbing, but at least it had been tempered with a veneer of urbanity. Now that veneer had gone and his blatant maleness seemed to threaten her more than ever.

'What do you want?' she asked, sounding every bit as flustered as she felt.

'I've come to look over the yard,' he drawled, slipping his hands in the pockets of his jeans. 'And there's certainly far more to see here than I thought.'

She mastered the feminine impulse to put a defensive hand to the bra of her bikini to make sure it was properly in place. But she could do nothing about the hot blush she knew had crept into her face. Amusement and appreciation were in Zack's blue eyes as he looked her over leisurely, lingering on her curves.

'The yard's closed on a Sunday, Mr Thole,' she said sharply. 'My hours are nine to five in the week and nine till one on Saturday. If you want to make an appointment between those times I'll be delighted to show you round. Till then...'

Zack caught hold of her by the arm, and the unexpected physical contact seemed to knock the breath out of her.

'And in the week I'm busy,' he said impatiently. 'I don't intend wasting time driving out of London from my office because your sunbathing takes priority over business.'

She bit back a sharp retort, because his words had reminded her of the importance of the transaction. She was about to tell him grudgingly that she'd show him round, when her defiant gaze met his. For a spell-binding instant Zack's blue eyes held hers, the atmosphere between them charged with a sexual static that was frightening and yet exciting, and which could only have one ending. And then suddenly the enclosed circle of sensual magic was broken by the loud chugging of a passing boat. Snatching her arm away from him as though his touch burned her, Eve said, her voice every bit as breathless as if she'd climbed ten flights of stairs, 'I'll get the keys to the boat-sheds, Mr Thole.'

'Fine, and while you're at it, maybe we could go back to first-name terms. Even when it's business, I don't like a lot of unnecessary formality.'

'Well, I do,' she retorted. 'It makes me feel...'

'Safer?' he supplied for her mockingly.

'No,' she denied, her voice cold as she glared at him. 'And I'm not sure I know what you mean by that, anyway.'

There was a pause and then Zack said pointedly, 'Sooner or later you are going to wear your luck out with that mixture of icy aloofness and smouldering fire.'

'Are you threatening me?' she asked with a slight lift of her chin.

Zack laughed, running his hand through his thick hair. It was clear that she amused and exasperated him in roughly equal parts.

'We'd better pick up on this conversation later,' he said drily. 'Right now, I'm here to look over the premises. Nothing else. Does that make you feel better?'

He spent about an hour inspecting the two acres which comprised the boatyard. Any element of flirtation between them was lost as he fired questions at her. Eve had retrieved her skirt at the same time as she'd fetched the keys. No longer disadvantaged by being half-naked with him, she put up a good show of answering his queries competently. Though he would probably have had very little patience with her, she thought drily, if she hadn't been able to supply him immediately with the information he wanted. Whatever the sparks that flew between them, when it came to financial dealings, Zack was as hard as nails.

They strolled back to the small riverside garden where Eve had been sketching before he'd driven up. She offered him a cold drink and they sat at the white slatted table while he completed his list of questions.

Why hadn't the charge for private moorings gone up in line with inflation? What reason had her father had for not selling off the last of the old hire-boats when they'd been replaced with newer models? Why was the rent so low for the sheds the boatyard let out to a marine trimmer and a rigger?

The implication was clearly that Zack believed the business was not being run to maximise profits, an implication that rankled with Eve. It was perfectly true that more income could be generated, especially with the leasing of some of the sheds, but her father disliked the way big business had bought many of the old boatyards on the river, selling off the less profitable parts in order to skim off the financial cream. To him, maintaining the longstanding friendly links they had with the craftsmen who'd worked on the site for years was more important than collecting the last penny on the leases. She was quick to point the fact out to Zack.

'For someone so independent, you have some surprisingly sentimental values,' he commented.

'I don't call them sentimental,' she answered. 'Profit is important, but so, too, is tradition. The boatyard was set up by my grandfather almost eighty years ago, and a couple of the businesses we lease out sheds to go back that far too.'

Zack gave her a speculative look and stretched his long legs out in front of him as he relaxed in the sun.

'Family's very important to you, isn't it?'

'Isn't it to you?' she countered.

He shrugged his broad shoulders, his gaze fixed at some distant point across the glinting river.

'My parents were divorced when I was fifteen. Divorce has a way of carving up any sense of tradition.'

There was a cynical note to his voice. He was thinking of a past that stirred memories it was still hard to look back on. Somehow it touched her in a way she couldn't define. She had judged Zack to be self-contained, very positive and with more than a touch of ruthlessness. Glimpsing beneath that, she felt a curious bond of closeness with him that meant it didn't seem at all intrusive to ask, 'Are you still bitter about it?'

'Bitter?' Zack seemed surprised. His blue eyes came back to her as he said casually, 'No, if anyone had the right to be bitter it was my mother. I'm just angry that my father could have treated her the way he did.'

'Why? What happened?'

Zack stood up and strolled a couple of steps towards the bank, hooking a thumb in the waistband of his jeans as he rested a foot on the concrete edge to the water.

'It wasn't too happy a marriage anyway,' he said with his back to her. 'My father wasn't the steady type, but my mother was very much in love with him. She used to work as the secretary for the manager of a bowling alley. My father never managed to hold down a job for any length of time. One Friday when she and the manager were taking the till money to the bank they were attacked by a couple of thugs. My mother had ammonia thrown in her face. For a while it looked as if she'd lose her sight completely. Specialist treatment saved her from going blind, but it left her very badly scarred.' There was a pause, and then Zack added in the same unemotional voice, 'That was when my father walked out on her. He said he couldn't bear to look at her.'

He put it bluntly, but the impact of the tragedy hit Eve too deeply for her to be able to murmur any immediate words of sympathy. Instead she asked quietly, 'How old were you?'

'I was thirteen. My sister Suzanne was eight. My mother waited two years and then got a divorce on the grounds of desertion. After my father walked out she took us to Poole and we lived with my grandparents. Which was where I first got a liking for messing about with boats,' he said, lightening the conversation as he turned back to her.

'Is your mother still alive?' Eve asked.

'No. She died when I was in my last year at university.' He took a deep breath and said, 'The one thing I really regret is that I didn't get the chance to make life easier for her. Money was very tight when I was growing up.'

'And your father? Do you ever see him?'

'He contacted me a while back,' Zack said briefly. 'I didn't want to know.' He sat down again and turned Eve's sketch-book towards him to look at the studies she'd made that morning. 'Do you always work on riverscapes?' he asked.

'Mostly,' she said, a wry note coming into her voice as she added without meaning to, 'It's a good commercial subject.'

Zack's intense blue eyes focused astutely on her.

'That doesn't sound like you,' he remarked.

'When it comes to painting, I know my limitations,' she said lightly, wanting to change the topic.

Zack flicked through her sketch-book and then asked with uncanny perceptiveness, 'Who told you your work was commercial?'

He was trespassing on her personal space again if he only knew it, and she said rather curtly as she took the sketch-book from him, 'Someone at art school.'

Zack's gaze narrowed on her. 'Your fiancé?' he asked.

She read the criticism in his voice and said defensively, 'Simon was very talented.'

'And very critical of everyone else,' he said, so that it sounded more like a statement than a question.

'You have a right to be critical when you're that good,' she said, her eyes warning him that he'd said enough.

'Nobody has the right to build themselves up by knocking somebody else down,' he replied levelly.

The brief interlude when she had stopped fencing with him had vanished as quickly as it had come. The usual force-field of tension vibrated between them again. Refusing to get into an argument with him, she didn't challenge his statement. Zack looked at her in his faintly amused, considering way, though his eyes were steadily intent.

Then he stretched out a hand to run his palm lightly over her shoulder.

'You're catching the sun,' he remarked easily. 'Pass me the cream and I'll put some on your shoulders for you.'

'I'll do it,' she said quickly.

He ignored her, reaching forward leisurely to pick up the tube of cream.

'You don't want to burn, do you?' he asked as he swept the hair off the nape of her neck and started to smooth the cream in rhythmic circles over her back.

Her heart was suddenly beating with heavy, rapid strokes. Deftly Zack slipped one strap off her shoulder, and she gasped and said in defensive alarm, 'What do you think you're doing?'

'Avoiding getting oil on your bikini,' he answered grittily. 'What do you think?'

She couldn't turn round, because if she did he'd see he had made her blush.

'You know,' he continued as he carried on the sweeping caressing movements of his hand, the lazy humour in his voice that she found so maddening, 'the way you act at times, anyone would think you'd never been touched by a man before.'

'Believe it or not,' she flared, pulling away and dragging her strap back over her shoulder, 'there are some women who prefer not to be touched by just anyone...'

'I was putting some cream on your shoulders,' he pointed out with diminishing patience, 'not trying to have my wicked way with you.'

'Really?' she said with cold disbelief as she got haughtily to her feet.

'Yes,' he said forcefully. 'But, just so that you realise it, let me show you the difference.'

Before she had the chance to evade him, his strong arms slid round her, drawing her tightly against him as he bent his head. Her world seemed to spin with the sheer unexpectedness of it. A tremor of fire darted along her nerves as she felt his lips part hers with a demand that was as gentle as it was determined. A wave of molten weakness went through her, so intense that she couldn't begin to attempt to save herself.

Zack shifted slightly to hold her still more intimately, and she moaned a protest deep in her throat, as he made her aware of his hard, aroused body. Shocked at the surge of wild pleasure that went through her, she struggled to break free, but Zack merely enveloped her more tightly in his arms as he deepened his exploration of her mouth.

To her utter dismay, she knew she was losing to the urgent need he was stirring in her to respond. Involuntarily she began to kiss him back, the movement of her lips complementing his. She was scarcely aware that his experienced hands had found and dealt with the fastening of her skirt. Her fingers tangled feverishly in the crisp hair at the nape of his neck, a shiver of frightening pleasure racing through her as she felt Zack's hands caressing the smooth length of her back.

He slid his palms up to her shoulder-blades before tracing them down again, his one hand slipping fluently under the band of her bikini briefs. The blaze of erotic sensation made her gasp, and in that instant she suddenly realised what she was allowing him to do.

She twisted free from his arms, her eyes blazing as she stared at him, her small breasts rising and falling rapidly.

'You really are quite something,' Zack drawled, his breathing as disturbed as her own. 'I don't know what turns me on more, your sudden flashes of temper, or those cool, provoking looks you give me from under those long, long eyelashes.'

'How dare you?' she breathed. 'How *dare* you kiss me like that? Don't you ever, ever touch me again.'

'Why?' he taunted. 'Are you afraid you're getting to like it? Because I'm certainly getting addicted!'

'You ever try that again,' she warned, 'and I'll slap you so hard I'll send you reeling!'

'Am I supposed to take that as another challenge?' he asked, his sensual mouth quirking with amusement as he took a step towards her.

A hot little shiver raced over her skin. She was shatteringly aware of the strength of his shoulders, the hard plane of his chest, the way he reminded her of a beautifully aligned and dangerous animal. Standing her ground with the greatest of difficulty, she flashed back, 'In case you've forgotten, I happen to be involved with someone else.'

'No, I hadn't forgotten. But a few seconds ago *you* seemed to have. It makes me wonder if you and your boyfriend match up sexually when you ignite with me the way you do...'

'Your mind never seems to rise above the topic of bed,' she said furiously, cutting him short. 'Well, for your information, Greg isn't interested in a woman just for her body the way you seem to be. And he's much too much of a gentleman to try and rush me into... into...'

She trailed off, her anger dissipated in her acute embarrassment that Zack had provoked her into such an intimate confession. She watched as slow incredulity came into Zack's blue eyes.

'Are you telling me that you've never... that your relationship with Greg is platonic?'

'That *is* how you'd class any relationship that ended short of bed, isn't it?' she snapped sarcastically.

Zack laughed shortly. 'And you say you love him.'

'I *do* love him,' she said vehemently.

'When you say he's—how did you put it?—too much of a gentleman to rush you?' he asked with deft derision, before going on, 'Don't you think if you loved him you might prefer it if he was a little less... gentlemanly?'

'You're too much of a cheap womaniser to begin to understand the meaning of the word "gentleman",' she stormed. 'I'm not surprised Greg couldn't work for you...'

'So he told you about that, did he?' Zack cut across her.

She was too angry to catch the tone of his voice that was stripped now of its amused contempt.

'Yes, he did,' she retorted heatedly.

'What else did Greg say?' Zack demanded, snatching hold of her wrist with such force that she gasped, startled out of her anger.

Zack's eyes raked hers. His brows were drawn together, emphasising the gaunt lines of his face.

'Let go of me,' she breathed indignantly. 'You're hurting my wrist.'

'Answer me,' Zack ordered curtly.

'He said you fired him,' she said, pulling her wrist away from him sharply as he released his grip on her.

'Was that all?' Zack asked less savagely.

'Yes,' she said resentfully. 'And now perhaps you'd stop interrogating me. You just get one thing clear, Mr Thole, our relationship is strictly business. And just because you're buying into the yard, it doesn't mean you have any rights over me.'

'What very quaint notions you have,' he said gratingly as he grabbed hold of her by the forearms and pulled her against his chest. 'I've never had to force a woman, or buy one. And, believe me, you'll be no different.'

The anger went out of his face, replaced by amusement as he saw the blaze of outrage that darkened her green eyes.

'Tell your father I'll contact him in the week. And as for you, my little elf, I'll see you later.'

She knew what retaliation would get her. Zack's eyes glinted with gentle laughter, as if he knew the effort it cost her to control her temper. He let her go, and as he walked away the impulse to throw something at him to relieve her pent-up hostility took hold of her and she snatched up the nearest thing to hand, a tube of Titanium White paint.

Instinct seemed to warn him, and he turned as she hurled it at him, catching it neatly. A smile tugged at his mouth as he weighed it for an instant in his hand as though debating what to do with it. Now that the flashpoint of her temper was passed, she was suddenly very relieved that she had provoked him to mirth by her action and not anger. Zack's eyes invited her to laugh as he tossed the tube of paint casually back to her.

She caught it and put it on the table, refusing to let him see how tempted she was to smile. Zack Thole was a playboy who never lost the opportunity to make a pass at a woman. However strong the pull of attraction she felt for him, what she wanted was emotional tranquillity and, above all, commitment. That put him effectively beyond the pale, and she hadn't put up such a fight with him earlier only to capitulate at the last to his sense of humour.

CHAPTER FIVE

EVE was checking through some booking forms in her office on Tuesday afternoon when her father walked briskly through the door.

'Hello, Dad!' she exclaimed delightedly.

'Hello, love,' Frank smiled, bending to kiss her. 'Well, how have you been getting on while I've been away?'

'Fine,' she laughed, chiding him gently as she added, 'And I did hope you'd be away longer. I thought you'd stay in Wroxham for the week. Dr Osborne said what you needed was rest. Remember?'

Frank patted her shoulder.

'I've had a rest. Now, stop worrying about me,' he teased.

Eve smiled and said, 'Well, you look better for the break.'

'Yes, I've had a good change of scene,' Frank said humorously, 'from cruisers on the Thames to cruisers on the Broads!' He glanced over her shoulder at the paperwork she was doing and asked, 'How are the bookings for this week?'

'We're doing well,' she said. 'In fact, we're so busy that I've been really glad of Robin to help out. He's on his way to Windsor at the moment to see to one of the boats. It's got some sort of trouble with its propellor.'

'I expect it's underwater fouling again,' Frank commented, before asking, 'Has Mr Thole been in touch?'

She felt herself colour slightly at the memory of her bikini-clad encounter with Zack the previous Sunday. Her voice was a shade too detached as she said, 'Yes, he's looked over the yard. There were a couple of points he'll probably want to raise with you, but overall I think he was reasonably impressed.'

'I'll give him a ring first thing tomorrow and let him know I'm back,' Frank said. 'I want this deal clinched as soon as possible.'

And, despite her dislike on a personal level of having Zack as a partner, Eve, too, wanted the agreement signed. With his financial backing to tide them over, perhaps her father would stop driving himself so hard.

The necessity for that became more imperative when Frank had a dizzy spell at the yard the next day. Eve realised his health was the reason he had cut short his stay in Wroxham. When she questioned him about it she told her Dr Osborne had arranged for him to go into hospital the next week for more tests.

Robin left for Greece the next Saturday. Eve had enjoyed having him around at home and at the boatyard. The demands of work and two men to look after hadn't given her much time to think about her relationship with Greg, and she had been quite glad to shelve the issue.

Now it came back to the forefront of her mind. She knew she wasn't happy with Greg in the way Deborah was happy with Stuart. And yet she couldn't help shying away from that kind of emotional submergence in a partnership. The risk of loving a man with no holding back carried with it the risk of betrayal and loss. She had what she wanted in her relationship with Greg. If she never experienced that sense of oneness with him, at least he would never make her feel the unbearable pain of being torn apart. So why didn't she agree to marry him?

As usual, she didn't come up with an answer. Fleetingly she wondered whether, if she hadn't met Zack, she might by now have been engaged to Greg. She dismissed the thought immediately. It wasn't Zack who was holding her back. It was memories of Simon.

As she got ready for her date with Greg on Saturday evening, she reprimanded herself sternly for her indecision. Five years was long enough to have got over a disastrous love affair. She paused as she braided her long hair into a stylish French plait, her eyes falling on her sketch-book that lay on the bed. She fastened her plait, threw it over her shoulder and went to sit on the bed.

Turning the cover of the sketch-book, she looked at one of her pastel drawings. Trivial and commercial had been how Simon had described her work. The assessment in itself hadn't been important. What did matter was that it showed his total contempt for her. For once the thought hurt less than it did usually. She even felt mild annoyance at his lofty judgement.

She turned the pages, trying to assess her efforts impartially. And then her hand froze. She had momentarily forgotten the sketch she had made of Zack from memory the other day. It was a monochrome portrait, and the likeness was striking.

She'd caught perfectly the glint of devilish humour in his eyes, the strong, hawkish lines of his face, the sensual yet firm mouth. The quizzical expression she had captured so perfectly mocked her. She hadn't meant to draw him, but her hand had seemed to have a will of its own. The feelings Zack aroused in her which she constantly denied had found expression in another form, and the creative impulse had without any doubt at all found its roots in sexuality.

Impatiently she ripped the page out of the sketch-book, intending to crumple it up into a ball. Instead she stopped, holding the torn-out page in her hand. *Was* Zack the reason why she still hadn't given Greg an answer to his proposal? Somehow she couldn't discount it, even though the idea seemed utterly insane. Yet the very last thing she wanted was any entanglement with a man who wasn't looking for a stable relationship and who could only cause her trouble if she allowed herself to become either emotionally or physically involved with him.

The doorbell rang and she hesitated, the sketch still in her hand. It was too good to tear up just because the subject matter galled her. Convinced that her motive had nothing to do with sentimentality, she slipped the drawing back inside the book and went downstairs to open the door to Greg.

'How very summery you look,' he commented approvingly as he bent to kiss her.

She was wearing a pale green skirt with a loose matching top that had a beaded and embroidered motif on the front. It was ideal for a warm summer evening, leaving her arms bare.

Greg drove them to one of the riverside pubs which had a terrace built along the bank and which was very popular during the summer months. They found a table near the stone balustrade and sat chatting while the pleasure-craft plied lazily up and down the Thames. The buzz of conversation and laughter came from the surrounding tables, adding to the placid feel of the evening. As the twilight deepened, mosquitoes danced over the water, promising yet another blazing, sultry day.

Everything seemed perfect, yet Eve was increasingly conscious of a sense of fatality she couldn't seem to shake off. The talking to she'd given herself earlier hadn't done one bit of good. No matter how hard she went on trying to persuade herself to the contrary, no matter how easy and relaxed she and Greg seemed to be together, what she felt for him wasn't deep enough for a lifetime commitment.

The realisation startled her. Dazed by the depressing clarity of her discovery, for an instant she lost track of what Greg was saying. She came back to the conversation as he asked, 'What would you like me to bring you back from New York this time while I'm away?'

She fingered the stem of her glass and shook her head.

'I don't expect you to buy me things,' she said with a nervous smile.

There was no point in delaying the inevitable. She was going to steel herself to tell him that she couldn't marry him.

'I like buying you things,' Greg said genially, taking hold of her hand. 'We're going to go a long way, you and I. And then I'm going to buy you everything and anything you've ever wanted. You're bright and attractive, and I reckon if you and I were to go into business on our own we'd make a real success of it.'

He caught her look of surprise and went on, 'I haven't mentioned it before, but it's what I've been planning on for quite some time. I want to go into management consultancy. We could work together as a team.'

This made what she had to say even harder. She didn't answer immediately, and he asked with a trace of impatience, 'What's wrong? Don't you like the idea?'

'I think the idea of your striking out on your own is great,' she said. 'It's just that... Greg, could we go somewhere quieter? There's something I've got to tell you.'

'You make it sound horribly ominous,' Greg joked, giving her a slightly puzzled look. 'Well, if you want to go somewhere quieter, let's stroll along the towpath a little way.'

They crossed the crowded terrace together and went down the stone steps that led to the rough, rutted path by the river. The noise of talk and laughter from the pub faded as they walked with the expanse of river on the one side and the resting wheat fields on the other.

A short distance ahead was a white gate barring the path. Greg waited till they had reached it before saying, 'OK, what is it you want to tell me?'

For an instant she stared at the broad meanders of the river that were the colour of pewter in the dusk, and then she looked back at him and said quietly, 'Greg, I'm sorry, but I can't be part of those plans you've got for the future.'

'Why not?' he said with a frown. 'Look, you've got business acumen and ambition. You're wasting your time working for your father in that cramped little office. Together you and I could be a real success story.'

'You sound as if you're looking for a business partner, not a wife.'

'I'm looking for both,' he told her.

As she drew breath to tell him as gently as she could that she couldn't fill either role, Greg took hold of her by the shoulders.

'Well?' he demanded.

'It's no use, Greg. It wouldn't work. I like you a lot. You know I do, but... but I can't marry you.'

For a second he looked so totally disbelieving that she hated herself for disappointing him. Then he smiled wryly and said, recovering his usual assurance, 'I suppose I should have known you'd turn me down at least once. But you ought to know by now I don't give up easily on anything I want.'

'Greg, I'm not going to change my mind...' she began.

'And I'm not going to change mine,' he countered. 'I want you as my wife, Eve.'

'Please don't make this harder. I know you think you can persuade me. I've been wrong to let you go on hoping for as long as I have, but...'

'Eve, don't be a fool,' he said forcefully, catching hold of her by the arm. 'We're perfect for each other.'

'No, we're not. You only think we are, but, if we married, neither of us would be happy for very long.' She paused, knowing that what she was about to say would sound hard, but it would be kinder than letting him believe he'd wear down her resistance in the end. 'Greg, I'm truly sorry,' she said miserably, 'but you're going to New York in a few days' time. Let's use that to make the break from seeing one another.'

His eyes hardened, and for a moment she glimpsed a deep and almost frightening anger in them. His fingers tightened painfully on her skin.

'You're sorry?' he repeated with harsh cynicism. 'You wreck all my plans and you say you're sorry!'

'Yes,' she said desperately. 'I didn't want to hurt you.'

'Well, that's very noble of you. Whatever happened to the "we'll still be good friends" line that's supposed to soften the blow? My God, you've kept me dangling for a whole damn year...'

'Greg, please,' she cut across him, her voice low and intense.

'"Greg, please,"' he mimicked savagely, pulling her to him, his face dark with fury as he bent his head.

'Stop it!' she gasped, turning her head away sharply.

He let her go with an abruptness that held both violence and contempt. Breathing hard, he stared at her.

'You bitch,' he said, before turning and walking purposefully back along the path.

Stunned, she called after him, her voice uncertain, 'Greg? Where... where are you going?'

He turned and said gratingly, 'I'm going home. And as for you, after leading me on the way you have all this time, you can damn well walk.'

She stared at him in complete astonishment. She didn't know whether to run after him or whether to stand her ground. Pride won. Disbelievingly, she stayed by the gate, watching as Greg continued walking without even a backward glance till the dusk swallowed him up.

She turned and leant her arms along the bar of the gate. Her throat felt tight. Gently came the wash of the river, emphasising the stillness. She was stunned and angry and upset. She couldn't believe that Greg had simply abandoned her. Was this how they'd ended the year they'd spent together?

A saying she remembered her mother using to describe a friend's husband flashed through her mind. 'A street angel but a house devil.' Did that describe Greg? All affability in public, but with a furious temper if she annoyed him when they were alone? Shaken, she wondered if she'd had a lucky escape.

She stayed for a while, resting against the gate, conscious of a faint stirring of relief. She could see now that this had been inevitable, but it didn't stop her from feeling bruised and sensitive. Rallying determinedly, she checked in her purse to make sure she had some tenpence coins for a phone. Then she walked soberly back to the pub to call her father to ask if he'd come to pick her up.

The saloon bar was crowded. Groups of people stood talking, strengthening the convivial atmosphere that was provided by the rustic décor with its low oak beams and large collection of gleaming brass.

She made her way towards the exit and then stopped in complete dismay. Coming straight towards her was Zack, and with him was a sophisticated blonde who looked far too airy and far too pretty. Eve had no chance to dodge them because they were almost on top of her. She could hardly credit the conspiracy of fate that had brought them into this pub. Abandoned by Greg as she was, Zack was the very last person on earth she wanted to run into.

'Well, surprise, surprise,' he greeted her in his well-modulated voice.

The faintly amused smile he gave her was infuriatingly attractive.

'Hello, Zack,' she said with commendable composure.

The low-ceilinged, crowded pub seemed to make the physical impact of his height and strength more disturbing. She noticed that he had his palm against the slim back of his companion.

So that was the type of woman who appealed to him, she thought almost crossly. Well, she might have guessed he'd go for the self-assured, elegant type.

In her early thirties, the other woman had the sort of cool poise that suggested she could be all allure when she was alone with a man. Her honey-blonde hair fell sleekly in a silky bob. Under its heavy fringe her eyes were grey, and fringed with long, blonde-tipped lashes. With her golden skin and white, safari-style dress, she had a Grace Kelly brand of class. Eve felt suddenly that her simple green two-piece lacked any sort of chic.

'Stephanie,' Zack said easily, 'this is Eve Hallam, a friend of mine.'

Was it her imagination, or did he succeed in shading the word friend very lightly with innuendo? If he did, Stephanie evidently didn't catch it, for she said with a deft rush of patronising friendliness that was meant to put Eve firmly in her place, 'Zack's mentioned you. You help out in the little boatyard he's investing in.'

'And you must be Zack's personnel manager,' Eve said smoothly, though her eyes held a dangerous sparkle.

She could see now why Deborah hadn't seemed to like Stephanie much when she had spoken about her at the party. Stephanie smiled and glanced up at Zack as though sharing a private joke with him. The meaning that flew between them was obvious. She was clearly very much more to Zack than an employee. Eve felt a quick surge

of anger at the confirmation of what she'd always suspected. This showed that he'd never been serious about
her.

'You and Greg must join us for a drink,' Zack said.

'I... Actually, I'm not with Greg,' Eve said boldly.
'I'm meeting a friend.'

It wasn't a good lie, but it was the best she could come
up with impromptu. There was no way she was going
to let Zack know that Greg had just walked out on her.

'It's getting rather late,' Stephanie said, glancing at
her slender wristwatch. 'Are you sure you haven't been
stood up?'

The slight smile made the delivery of the remark
perfect.

'No, I think it's more likely he's gone to the wrong
pub,' Eve said, trying not to glare at Stephanie. 'Perhaps
he thought I meant the George instead of the George
and Dragon.'

'Then have a drink with us while you wait,' Zack said,
a hint of amusement in his eyes as though he appre-
ciated Eve's inventiveness. 'I know Stephanie's will be
a crème de menthe. What will you have, Eve?'

She couldn't very well refuse. Knowing he had out-
manoeuvred her, and suspecting him of doing it deliberately, she said coolly, 'I'll have a Bezique.'

'With ice?' he asked, and this time she knew she didn't
imagine the faint mockery.

'Yes, lots of it,' she said, her eyes warring with his.

While he went to the bar, Stephanie looked around
languidly for a table.

'I think there's room over in the corner,' she said,
hitching her shoulder-bag more securely in place as she
moved between the tables with a model's walk. Eve cast
a wistful glance in the direction of the exit and the pay-
phones and then followed her.

Stephanie squeezed on to the banquette and then said, as Eve sat down opposite her, raising her voice a little above the background of conversation, 'How absolutely awful for you to be kept waiting like this by your date. I'd feel so horribly conspicuous if I had to sit all alone in a pub. Not that I've ever had to. Aren't you afraid of having passes made at you?'

'Oh, I can look after myself,' Eve said lightly, her restraint more than taxed.

'Heavens, you're not one of these ardent feminists, are you?' Stephanie trilled.

Eve thought it would be easier to keep her temper if she didn't answer, and Stephanie went on, 'Well, perhaps that sort of independence appeals to some men. I'm more old-fashioned.' She glanced up as Zack joined them with their drinks and added, flirting gently, 'I much prefer having someone around to look after me.'

Zack sat down on the banquette beside her and put a casual arm round her shoulders.

'Stephanie,' he said, his voice amused as he contradicted her, 'you are one of the most capable women I know.'

Stephanie laughed and snuggled against him while Eve, outwardly unruffled, was consumed by a blaze of hot, irrational jealousy. At that moment she would have derived the most intense pleasure from tipping Stephanie's crème de menthe down her pristine white dress. And as for Zack, well, if he so much as even tried to lay a hand on her ever again, he'd see what he got for it! Her furious thoughts were interrupted by him.

'How's that painting coming along that you were working on last Sunday?'

Determined not to show that she had any recollection of the blood-rushing intimacy with which he had kissed her that day, she said distantly, 'It's shaping up nicely.'

Zack's blue eyes narrowed on her face.

'When you've finished it, I'd like to buy it.'

She was tempted to retort that she'd sooner burn it than let him have it. Stephanie gave a little laugh and said protestingly, 'But, Zack, you don't collect amateur paintings.'

He brushed her temple with his lips and Eve's eyes grew stormier still.

'My charming ignoramus. Eve isn't an amateur.'

'I'm afraid I don't sell my paintings privately,' she informed him. 'Only through the gallery in Marlow.'

Zack removed his arm from Stephanie and said, 'Make an exception.'

It wasn't an order, but it sounded like one. Despite Stephanie's presence, they might have been alone for the dangerous sparks of confrontation between them. Eve was about to defy him with a flat refusal when someone carrying drinks to another table knocked clumsily into theirs.

Quite how it happened Eve didn't see, but Stephanie's hand was on her glass and somehow the drink went over, spilling into her lap. In the crowded pub the person who had caused the mishap moved on, apparently unaware of what had happened.

'Damn!' Stephanie breathed angrily. 'My God, just look at my dress! Wouldn't you think people would be more careful?'

Zack righted the glass and immediately handed her his handkerchief.

'If it's ruined, I'll have to buy you another.'

Stephanie put her hand up to his strong jaw and kissed him lightly.

'You're sweet to me,' she purred, before standing up and saying, 'I'd better go and splash some cold water on my dress. It feels horribly sticky.'

Left alone with Zack, Eve hurriedly finished her drink. He leant back, watching her lazily before commenting, 'It doesn't look as if your friend's going to show up.'

She checked her watch.

'No, it doesn't,' she agreed crisply, picking up her shoulder-bag. 'I don't think I'll wait any longer. It was nice of you to let me join you, but I feel as if I'm intruding.'

Something flickered in Zack's eyes. Then he asked bluntly, 'How long have you been two-timing Greg?'

'I have not been...'

She broke off and Zack said smoothly, 'This is most intriguing. I always suspected you to be a woman of mystery. So who is it exactly you'd arranged to meet?'

'I don't see that's any of your business,' she told him. 'And now I've got to be going.'

'I'll walk you to your car.'

For an instant she stared at him. It wasn't possible that he knew what had happened between her and Greg this evening. Yet she had the distinct feeling that if he didn't actually know, he strongly suspected. Damn him, she thought, he probably found this amusing. But if the glitter in his eyes was amusement it seemed very dry.

'Please don't bother,' she said dismissively, unable to resist adding, 'If Stephanie comes back from the cloakroom and finds you're not here, she'll wonder where you are. And she's already told me how much she hates being in a pub without a man for protection.'

To her intense annoyance Zack laughed, his eyes under his hawkish brows alight with knowing humour.

'I can see you've taken to Stephanie,' he commented. 'But anyway, she'll be a few minutes getting the stain out of her dress.' He saw Eve search for an answer and asked, 'You *do* have your car with you, don't you?'

'As a matter of fact, Dad dropped me off,' she said, feeling the betraying colour come into her face.

'So how do you intend getting home?' he asked.

'I'm going to walk!' she snapped, getting to her feet.

'To Cookham? In those sandals?' he asked as he stood up.

'It would be preferable to being given a lift by you,' she flashed back, unable to curb her temper any longer.

'Are you disappointed that with Stephanie present I won't be able to kiss you goodnight?'

'You are insufferable!' she breathed.

'And your haughty independence is starting to bug me,' he said, his humour vanishing, so that the static between them became more marked.

They were interrupted by Stephanie, who came up to them and said petulantly as she pulled at her wet skirt, 'I'm just about soaked, and I still haven't completely got the mark out. Zack, can we go home and I'll try and get it out there?'

'Sure,' Zack agreed.

'I do hope your date turns up,' Stephanie said sweetly to Eve as she tucked her hand through Zack's arm.

'I'm not waiting any longer,' she said. 'Zack's offered to give me a lift home.'

It was rewarding to see the look of annoyance that spread across Stephanie's face. But she quickly recovered herself. Nestling against Zack, she whispered audibly as Eve followed them out of the pub, 'I think you're developing a soft spot for this little waif.'

Eve didn't catch Zack's reply, but Stephanie evidently found it amusing. Smarting with a mixture of anger and humiliation, she walked a pace behind them as they crossed the dark car park. To have to be driven home by Zack and his superior girlfriend was the final touch to the most miserable evening. She felt that if she had to endure watching Stephanie flirt with him in her enticing, languid way any longer she'd explode with temper.

Zack opened the passenger door for Stephanie, while Eve got in the back. She might have not been in the car, for the way Stephanie managed to exclude her from the conversation. It was only as they took a left turn that she asked sharply, 'I thought you were going to drop Eve off first.'

'No, I thought I'd give you a chance to change out of that wet dress. I'll run Eve home then I'll come back.'

'You mean, when I've slipped into something more comfortable?' Stephanie teased softly, touching his sleeve with a caressing hand.

In the back of the car Eve folded her arms and stared out of the window, her eyes becoming even more mutinous when Zack laughed and said, 'Sounds promising.'

He pulled into a kerb outside a block of prestigious-looking flats. Eve would have thought that Stephanie could have managed to have walked the short distance to the porticoed entrance alone, but Zack evidently thought it more chivalrous to accompany her. The two of them stood for a moment with the light from the flats behind them. And then Stephanie's hands crept up coaxingly to his shoulders.

Eve, who hadn't meant to be watching, saw Zack glance at her. For an instant her stormy gaze clashed with his before he deliberately bent his head to kiss Stephanie. Eve looked away sharply. She could never remember being so hotly and furiously angry, nor work out why her emotions were so alarmingly extreme. It would have been reassuring to assume it had something to do with delayed reaction from splitting up with Greg, only she knew that wasn't so.

A moment later Zack opened the back door, and resting a hand against the frame, said casually, 'Hop in the front and I'll drive you home.'

She stared at him with intense hostility and he added mockingly, 'You'll be quite safe. I'm not going to bite you.'

She refused to rise to the gibe. While he walked round to the driving seat she moved to get in alongside him, maintaining a dignified silence. Determined that he wouldn't know that seeing him with another woman had evoked any reaction from her whatsoever, she began calmly as he started the engine, 'Did Dad tell you the work on *Rebel Lady* is almost finished now?'

Zack shot her a narrowed, slightly quizzical glance before answering.

'Yes, he mentioned it when we met to discuss the last of the legal formalities of the new partnership agreement.'

Eve, who was still simmering with resentment, deliberately kept the conversation centered on the boatyard as he drove. With a stab of satisfaction she saw that her cool, formal politeness was starting to needle him. Well, if he thought he'd succeeded in angering her by kissing Stephanie, she was proving conclusively how very wrong he was. In fact, it was pleasing her greatly to see that she was beginning to aggravate him. Yet her satisfaction wasn't without a slight edge of apprehension. Between her and Zack were the sort of undercurrents that made any type of provocation, however subtle, spiced with a hint of danger.

They were driving along a darkened country road, the Jaguar's powerful headlamps silvering the hedgerows, when Zack swung the car into a passing-point.

'Why...why have we stopped?' she demanded accusingly, instinctively edging away from him.

'Because,' he said with quiet ferocity, 'you and I are going to have a little talk.'

'What do you mean?'

'I mean you're going to tell me what happened between you and Greg tonight.'

'I've told you, I wasn't with Greg.'

Zack draped an arm lazily along the back of her seat and said, recapping her story, his tone emphasising its implausibility, 'I remember. You'd arranged to meet a friend, apparently at some time around ten o'clock, but he'd got muddled between the George and the George and Dragon although there isn't a pub called the George within...'

'You don't have any right to interrogate me,' she flared, cutting him short. 'And what's more, if you had the slightest notion of the word tact, you'd leave the topic alone. I suppose it would never occur to someone of your great sensitivity that I might be upset about Greg walking...'

She broke off and he said curtly, 'Go on.'

'All right,' she retorted. 'Greg left me stranded at the pub tonight. Now are you satisfied?'

'Well, he doesn't change, does he?' Zack muttered in a cynical undertone.

Not quite catching it, she demanded, 'What did you say?'

'I said, you don't seem very broken-hearted.'

'Well, I wouldn't pick your shoulder to cry on even if I were,' she retaliated. 'And although this may come as a surprise to you, I don't go about letting everybody see how I feel.'

'No?' he mocked softly. 'I got the impression that at times you very much let the lid off your feelings.'

She coloured at his reminder of how ardently she had kissed him on more than one occasion.

'That's the sort of cheap, detestable line I'd expect from you,' she told him as he started the car and pulled on to the road, before accelerating with a roar of controlled power.

'So what do you plan doing with your life now you and Greg have split up?' Zack asked, her anger glancing off him, apparently without effect.

'I'm going to settle for staying single,' she snapped.

Zack laughed softly.

'No, that won't do,' he said.

'And why not?' she demanded, thankful that they were fast approaching Cookham and couldn't discuss this much longer. 'I suppose,' she continued scathingly, 'it would be beyond your egotistical comprehension to have ever thought that there *are* women who can get along very happily even if their life doesn't revolve around some man.'

'Some women, maybe,' he agreed crisply, 'but not you.'

'I'm not going to continue this conversation,' she said hurriedly, sensing that she was on highly dangerous ground.

It occurred to her that where Zack was concerned she never felt entirely safe. The sexual awareness that had been between them from that first night seemed to be developing into a smouldering tension that might snap at any moment.

She saw him slant a quick, deliberately raking glance at her, and then he said, 'You were made to be part of a man's life. You're as sensual as a woman can be, Eve. There's enough fire in you for only one spark to set it alight. In fact, perhaps it's time I reminded you of that.'

'You just dare,' she breathed, her heart knocking against her ribs.

'There's very little I wouldn't dare where you're concerned,' he warned. 'And if you think you're cut out to be single, then you don't know the first thing about yourself.'

'Well, I know it would be preferable to being married to anyone like you,' she retaliated all the more vehemently because the atmosphere between them was so full of menacing static. 'In fact, I'd pity any woman who was unfortunate enough to be your wife!'

She stopped, breathing hard, aghast that in her anger she could have been so thoughtless. For an instant she had forgotten that Zack had been married and that his wife was dead. Her hands were trembling, and she clenched them together as she glanced at him.

Zack's eyes were intent on the road ahead. His jaw was tight, the grimness of his profile emphasising the lean, strong lines of his face. Eve bit her lip.

'I'm sorry,' she breathed. 'That was a hateful thing to say.'

'Forget it,' he said curtly.

There was a short silence. She sensed rather than saw the glance he gave her. Then he said, a spark of gentle humour in his voice, 'Don't look so contrite.'

She raised her eyes and falteringly returned his smile. The tension between them had shattered, replaced by a strange mood of clarity and understanding.

'How long were you married?' she asked quietly as Zack turned into her road.

'Three years,' he answered levelly.

There was a pause and then Eve asked, 'What happened?'

'There was... an accident.'

He pulled up outside her house and for a moment which to Eve seemed timeless his eyes held hers. Then, gently, he drew her into his arms, his mouth finding and parting hers with a tenderness that sent a wave of fire and weakness sweeping through her. As naturally as if she came into his arms every day, she slid her hands to his neck, letting him mould her to him as he deepened the kiss with a fierce, tender urgency that filled her with an aching hunger. All conscious thought seemed to have deserted her. She only knew that his exploration of her mouth was making her long for more.

She made a soft sound in her throat as the pleasure suddenly intensified. She felt Zack's hand slip to the softness of her breast and, shocked by the blaze of pleasure, she broke the kiss. Her eyes were feverish and bewildered as she stared at him, and then, totally confused by the madness that seemed to take hold of her whenever he touched her, she pushed open the car door and stumbled out.

'Eve...' Zack's voice was urgent and imperative.

But she didn't stop. She fled up the path, her emotions in turmoil. It was only after she'd let herself in and was leaning weakly against the closed front door, breathing as rapidly as if she'd had the narrowest of escapes from danger, that her thoughts steadied enough for her to realise why instinctively she'd run from him.

He was kissing and caressing her when he planned to drive back to Stephanie's, presumably to spend the night there. She heard Zack's car start with a surge of acceleration, but the anger she felt wasn't nearly as intense as the sharp, aching pain under her ribs, a feeling she had vowed she would never experience over any man again.

CHAPTER SIX

FRANK was admitted into one of the London hospitals for a series of tests the next week. Getting the partnership agreement with Zack finalised and signed beforehand had clearly been a weight off his mind. With Robin still away on holiday, for a while the management of the boatyard was to be left completely in Eve's hands. She half expected Zack would call in to check that she was capable of handling the responsibility, but he didn't, which was just as well, because she was still simmering with anger over his blatant involvement with Stephanie.

Eve could only suppose that the reason why Zack was still sending her flowers every day was because she represented some sort of challenge to his male ego. From what Deborah had told her, Zack evidently wasn't used to a woman who could remain immune indefinitely to his masculine charisma. Her conviction that she was completely beyond his reach mollified her a little, until she remembered how ardently she had kissed him. Impatient with herself, she pushed Zack resolutely from her thoughts. She had far too many pressing problems to deal with at work to be wasting time speculating about a man who could have no serious part to play in her life. Because even if Zack was serious about her, which he clearly wasn't, on the rebound from Greg she wasn't ready to begin another relationship.

As she drove into the yard on Saturday morning she saw that *Rebel Lady* was being pushed out from one of the repair sheds and let gently down the grooved slipway into the river. The cruiser was all sleek lines and gleaming woodwork, and if it had been any other customer's boat Eve would have paused to admire it. But she disliked the way it reminded her that Zack was now a partner in the business. In fact, she disliked any reminder of Zack at all. Her heels tapping smartly on the concrete, she made her way briskly to her office.

Saturday was always busy and, with so many customers calling in, the morning was hectic. Normally she finished work at lunch time on a Saturday, but today there was no chance of that. It was almost three o'clock, and she had just finished showing a Danish party over the cruiser they were hiring for the week, when she saw Zack's Jaguar turn into the boatyard. She stepped ashore from the cruiser's stern and on to the landing-stage as he got out of the car. Behind her the water churned as the cruiser pulled away and headed out into the river.

Zack came towards her and, as always, she was slightly jolted by his male attractiveness. He was wearing jeans and a yellow T-shirt. His tough stamina and physique made her feel disturbingly petite and feminine.

He joined her, indicating *Rebel Lady* which was moored beyond the slipway as he said naturally, as though they were picking up on a conversation, 'She looks good, doesn't she?'

And so do you. The thought came before she could suppress it. She wondered why Stephanie wasn't with him. Undoubtedly they would be spending the evening together, if not the entire night. Resentment against his effrontery in kissing her so intimately flared up, and she answered, her voice distinctly cool, 'The men have done a good job on her.'

Zack stabbed a glance at her. His blue eyes were uncomfortably direct, but she refused to drop her own. Faint quizzical amusement came into his gaze, and then he said, his manner impersonal and authoritative, 'I'd like to take her for a short trip to see how the engine's running before I settle the account.'

'I'm sure you'll find the work's been done satisfactorily,' she said more coldly still, letting him see that she resented his implication.

'Well, as you're the boss round here at the moment, if it's not, you'll be the one I'll complain to. So you'd better come with me.'

Anticipating her reaction, he caught hold of her wrist and warned, 'Tell me I can talk to one of the engineers, and I'll carry you on board over my shoulder.'

'You wouldn't dare,' she breathed furiously, struggling to pull away.

'Do you want to test me on it?' he asked with maddening calm.

'Let go of me this minute!' she demanded as he marched her on board. 'If you don't, I'm going to call one of the men.'

Zack let go of her.

'Do you mean one of *our* joint employees?' he mocked. 'I'd have thought you knew that it's only good management to present a united front.'

'Do you get a kick out of provoking me?' she asked angrily.

'I get a kick out of you, full stop.'

She was still hunting for a frosty put-down to his lazily amused remark when he started the engine. He swung the cruiser out into the river, setting the boats moored by the landing-stage rocking in its powerful wake.

In a slim linen skirt and softly pleated blouse, Eve wasn't dressed for a river trip, and in any case, she hotly resented his coercion. Plus, on top of that she didn't feel the least bit safe with him. The atmosphere between them seemed to have become more highly charged with every meeting. And not even her frosty politeness seemed to be an adequate defence against it any longer.

In spite of herself, she noted the strong, attractive lines of his face as he steered the cruiser up-river. Everything about the man seemed to threaten her. He was too male, too authoritative and too determined.

But the boat was a beauty, and when a minute or two later Zack glanced at her to say easily, 'Do you want to take her?' she couldn't resist the impulse to accept his offer.

They headed gently up the river that was smooth and wide in the lazy afternoon sun. To the left, stately houses with white-framed conservatories and elegant boat-houses brought their well-manicured lawns down to the water's edge, while to the right was the towpath. On the bank, some people were picnicking leisurely.

'She handles very well,' Eve said evenly as she handed the wheel back to him before asking with a perceptible shading of antagonism, 'Are you satisfied?'

'Yes, with the work.'

She wasn't sure what he meant by the remark. She gave him a wary glance, and to emphasise his point he added, 'I'm not trying to find fault with the yard, Eve.'

'Well, it sounded as if you were,' she replied coolly. 'But if you're not, can we go back now?'

'In a while,' he agreed.

She realised she was completely in his control and, disliking the idea intensely, she flared, 'Believe it or not, I'm extremely busy.'

'But never too busy to be thoroughly argumentative.'

'I don't get into arguments, except with you,' she told him.

'I wonder why that is,' he mocked.

She bit back a heated answer with the greatest of difficulty. And then only because some intuitive sense of self-preservation warned her that losing her temper might be a naked spark in the energy field of sexual tension that pulsed between them.

'You know,' Zack commented after a short silence, 'you're becoming so very controlled, I'm increasingly tempted to do something about it.'

'What do you mean?' she asked, knowing that she sounded flustered.

'You know exactly what I mean, but pretending to misunderstand me is just another annoying little trick you've developed lately,' he said, flicking a hard glance at her.

He brought the cruiser into the bank where trees cast dappled shadows over the towpath. In the distance, away from the lazy meanders of the river, the fields rose away to low, blue-tinged hills, while above was a blue sky swept with bold streaks of cloud.

Zack cut the engine and there was stillness. With a start of apprehension Eve realised that they were beyond the safety of houses and other people, and that she was as alone with him as she had been that night at Deborah's party.

'Well, that took some doing,' Zack commented, 'but I've finally got you to myself.'

'Do you make a habit of abducting women?' she asked with all the more hauteur because it seemed her only protection against him.

'What I make a habit of,' he said curtly, 'is going after what I want. And right now that happens to be you.'

She backed away from him as he took a step nearer.

'You stay away from me,' she breathed, her eyes blazing and her heart racing with a mixture of anticipation and alarm. 'Don't you dare lay a hand on me.'

'Because if I do I might feel how your pulse leaps?' he asked harshly, his arm snaking round her waist.

She hit out at him ineffectually before he imprisoned her tightly against him and bent his mouth swiftly to find hers. She pushed at him, making no impression at all as his mouth parted hers in a searching, demanding kiss. Her mind was already spinning in confusion, the arousal of his hard male body making tongues of dangerous fire leap along her veins. Her struggles died, and immediately Zack changed the kiss to one of slow, sensual demand. Eve's slim hands clutched at his shoulders and then crept around his neck. For a long moment she kissed him back ardently, acknowledging her feelings for him, before she even realised what she was doing.

And then sanity and memories of Stephanie returned and she twisted out of his arms, her face flushed and her heart beating wildly. Furious that she should have responded to him when he was sleeping with another woman, she raised her hand instinctively and slapped him. Zack swore and snatched hold of her wrist. His eyes glittered and he was breathing hard as he ordered angrily, 'Eve, cut the pretence.'

'What pretence?' she retaliated with a show of spirit, determined that he wouldn't know she was in love with him.

'The pretence that you don't want to go to bed with me.'

For an instant she was totally speechless. She coloured hotly, both with anger and with a sexual response to his intimate suggestion made her more furious still.

'You . . . you arrogant, conceited chauvinist!' she exploded. 'Just because your purring personnel manager can't wait for the opportunity to leap into bed with you, it doesn't mean . . .'

'Just because what?' Zack cut across her.

'How naïve do you think I am?' Eve stormed. 'Stephanie could hardly keep her hands off you. And you most certainly weren't going back to her flat for coffee and a game of Scrabble!'

To her fury, she saw amusement come into his eyes.

'Stop laughing at me,' she raged.

'Then stop being so damned amusing,' he ordered, before saying, 'I went back to Stephanie's flat that night solely to go through a couple of business matters.'

Eve glared hot disbelief at him.

'I suppose this explains why you ran away from me the other night when I kissed you,' he said.

'I've never run away from any man in my life!' she said hotly.

Zack caught hold of her insistently by the shoulders and almost shook her.

'Now listen, you little fury. I did not sleep with Stephanie that night. Nor have I ever slept with Stephanie.'

'You kissed her!'

'To make you jealous.'

'To make...?' Eve began falteringly, her anger waning as she looked up into his eyes.

'Yes,' he said forcefully. 'Stephanie was asking for it, so I thought I'd gauge your reaction.'

It was a dangerous and telling moment. Eve seemed unable to drag her gaze away from him. In every inch of her she was aware of Zack as a man and of the attraction that pulsed between them. If she didn't make some attempt to resist him now, it would be too late. Breathlessly she said, 'I'm not interested in your love-life.'

She expected Zack to fire a comment back at her. But he didn't, and she flashed a puzzled glance at him. She saw that his jaw was set determinedly, and his face had a hawkish keenness about it that she knew too well for her own comfort. She was about to state that she wanted to head back down-river, when he said with the sort of level, emphatic calm that eventually produced results, 'Now that we've got that cleared up, let's start this conversation again. Eve, why won't you get involved with me?'

'Why should I get involved with you?' she answered.

'Because I didn't imagine what was between us the night of the party. And I certainly haven't imagined the way you've kissed me.'

She wanted to flash back with another angry, defiant answer, but Zack was watching her with a gentle scrutiny that made her heart suddenly lurch strangely. She couldn't marshal her defences against him, because he'd stopped being the arrogant outsider who'd bought into the business and who had marched her aggressively on board. The magic was back, and she almost confessed that the reason why she'd been so hostile with him all along was because deep emotional commitment frightened her. It was much easier to keep denying that she had fallen in love with him.

Zack was quick to sense the change in her. He came and enfolded her in his arms, brushing her hair with his lips a_ his hands gently caressed her back. As if compelled by a force stronger than herself, Eve turned her face into his shoulder. Then, alarmed by the kindling of desire that was stirring so rapidly inside her, she pulled away. Zack let her go.

'Listen,' he said quietly, 'you don't have to put up defences against me. What makes you cling so desperately to your independence?'

She kept her head bent and didn't answer. Zack came and stood beside her, his hand fondling her shoulder before he kissed the nape of her neck and turned her gently but insistently towards him.

'I'm not in this for some kind of affair, Eve,' he said. 'You must know by now, I'm serious about you.'

She shook her head. If only she could have gone on fencing with him, this wouldn't be happening. But his change of tactic had made her totally vulnerable.

'Eve, tell me,' Zack insisted. 'Is it because of your fiancé that you won't give yourself to anyone?'

'Yes, but it's not quite the way you think,' she said in a hushed voice.

'Tell me.'

'I can't,' she whispered unhappily. 'I've never told anyone. It's just that I should never have become engaged to Simon. I should never... Oh, God!' she said with sudden desperation. 'It was all such a nightmare.'

Zack gathered her into his arms, holding her close. Then, when at last she looked up at him, he took her face in his hands and kissed her. It was a sweet, tender kiss and she knew beyond any doubt that he was telling her he loved her, because it was there in the way he touched her and held her. It was there in the depths of his blue eyes.

Against Zack's protectiveness, the pain of remembering eased. Suddenly she wanted to tell him, because doing so was a way of putting the past completely behind her. And she understood now that her future and her destiny lay entwined with Zack's.

She moved away from him a little and began, her voice quiet and pitched a shade low, 'Simon was killed in a car crash. It was very late when the hospital rang the flat where I was living. They said he was very critically ill. I got there as fast as I could but... but when I arrived...' She paused to keep her voice steady. 'Simon was already dead. When I finally left the hospital I ran into Leanne in the foyer. She was a second-year student. I didn't know her all that well...'

'Go on,' Zack prompted gently.

Eve drew a deep breath and continued, her voice more cramped, 'Leanne had been in the accident with Simon, but she'd been lucky enough to escape with only minor cuts. I thought he must have been giving her a lift home... but... Leanne was hysterical with shock. She started to scream at me what Simon had kept so carefully hidden. He'd been having an affair with her. To him I was only a second-rate talent whose family had made money. The boatyard was earning good profits five years ago. Simon's parents weren't well off. It seemed he wanted a rich wife to support him while he made his name in the art world. But it was Leanne he loved. He'd been sharing her bed the whole time, and I'd never even suspected. They'd been arguing when the car went off the road because... because she thought she was pregnant by him.'

'And was she?'

'She left art school at the end of the term. I heard afterwards she'd had an abortion.'

Zack drew her against him.

'Well,' he said, a note of harsh contempt in his voice, 'your fiancé certainly knew how to mess up people's lives.'

Strangely, she felt no desire to defend Simon. She realised she was finally over him.

'What made it so hard,' she said quietly as she turned her face against Zack's substantial shoulder, 'was that I couldn't grieve for him properly. I felt so betrayed.'

Zack smoothed her hair with a caressing hand.

'So that's why you've been putting up such a fight against me,' he said.

'I don't want to fall in love again,' she whispered.

'Do you think you have a choice?' he asked, a hint of humour in his voice. 'Haven't you realised yet that there hasn't been a choice for either of us?'

She looked up at him, her answer and the last of her old independence vanishing as her eyes met the twin blue flames in his.

'Eve, I promise you,' he said, his tone altering to become resolute and intense, 'no man's ever going to hurt you again.'

His gaze held hers before he tilted her chin and bent his head slowly, kissing her with an infinite gentleness. The only contact between them was his hand that shaped her face and his mouth on hers, but the tantalising sweetness of it made a quiver of desire run through her. Her fingers instinctively encircled his strong wrist as she kissed him back, long and confessingly.

'Trust me, Eve,' he whispered huskily as his mouth left hers. 'Forget Simon. Forget any part of you ever belonged to him.'

His fingers opened her palm and he pressed his lips to it with a tenderness that made her weak. She drew a ragged breath, her body aching for more of this drugging pleasure, unable to resist the heady seduction of his touch.

'I do trust you,' she breathed, slipping her arms up around his neck and tangling her fingers in his crisp hair as he began to kiss her fiercely and without any restraint.

'Oh, God, Eve,' he muttered at last against her cheek. 'I've wanted to kiss you and hold you like this from that very first moment.'

She smiled, her hands stroking his hair. With a low groan, his arms tightened around her. His lips found hers again in another demanding kiss that made a shock of desire race through her. He held her intimately, making her aware of his arousal, his mouth exploring hers with a thoroughness that made a wild need possess her to feel him throughout every inch of her.

Her heart was pounding when he finally raised his head.

'Enchantress,' he breathed as he slanted ardent, sipping kisses down her throat.

She closed her eyes with the feverish pleasure. For an instant she had the sensation that the cruiser had moved, making her balance unsteady, until she realised he had swept her off her feet. Dazed, she opened her eyes as Zack carried her into the foreward cabin.

The sight of the double bunk made comprehension shock her into an awareness of what must happen if she continued responding to him.

'Zack, no,' she whispered. 'I can't. You're going too fast for me.'

'I've waited for you long enough,' he breathed raggedly as he laid her gently on the bed.

He arched her to him with one strong arm while he leant over her, kissing her with a relentless hunger, his hand lightly stroking her thigh and waist before caressing her breast. A shudder racked her as his thumb found her taut nipple and, before she could begin to recover from the wild, frenzied pleasure, his fingers dealt efficiently with the buttons of her blouse.

'No,' she moaned faintly, the tide of sensation so agonisingly sweet that she didn't know whether she was protesting that he must stop, or pleading with him to continue.

'Yes, it's all right,' Zack breathed harshly, slipping her blouse smoothly from her shoulders and unclipping her bra. 'You want me, too. You know you do. It's why you're trembling, why your eyes are feverish and as green as emeralds.'

Her slim hands gripped his shoulders helplessly as he bent his head to press kisses on her bare skin while his strong, deft fingers stroked the soft swell of her naked breasts. She gave a husky cry as his mouth captured her nipple, his tongue tantalising it expertly to an arousal that made daggers of frenzied wanting shudder through her.

Breathlessly she murmured his name, her hands sliding under his T-shirt. She felt a convulsion rack him as her fingers ran down his spine. He pulled his shirt off and threw it aside, pressing her breasts to the hard plane of his chest as he kissed her again with a deep, raw passion.

She had no thought of drawing back now. This was the inevitable conclusion to the vibrations of sexual magnetism that had paired them together from the very first moment they'd met. She shivered as she felt Zack's weight, a feverish excitement driving her with a need to touch and explore the lean, hard perfection of his naked body.

Zack slid his palms down the whole length of her, his lips and hands making love to every part of her body as he expressed his delight in her. He girdled her waist with kisses before pushing her hair off her face to slide his mouth along the line of her jaw and down her throat. His body seemed to be enveloping her, his deep, husky voice mesmerising her as he told her again and again how beautiful she was, how she intoxicated him. He was driving her to delirium with his tantalisingly slow, erotic play.

The waves of sensation were so fierce and intense that she knew she could only trust to him to save her. She cried out his name as Zack allowed the pitch of pleasure to subside a little before tautening it inexorably to an exquisite agony so blinding, she felt she couldn't bear it.

She arched against him, on fire for him to take her. And then she gave a faint, choked sob as Zack entered her. She leapt with the slight pain of his first penetration, but she was too close to the surging peak of ultimate pleasure to be aware of anything but the dazzling beauty of unity with him. For an instant, as her hands gripped his shoulders, her eyes flew open to meet the driving, dark passion in his. And then she closed them again tightly, the violent storm of sensation gathering as she complemented his movements, until suddenly there was a shattering of all bonds. She tensed and cried out. Zack's deep groan of fulfilment came less than a second later as she was falling through darkness into a dazed and wondering freedom.

Afterwards she lay unmoving, her heart thudding and her body throbbing with the last widening ripples of response. Her eyes were still closed, and suddenly, as she felt the conquering strength of Zack's body move from hers, she wanted to weep helpless tears in reaction to his complete possession of her. He drew her into his arms and slowly her breathing became less uneven as he held her to him, his hands cherishing her, conveying a silent message of love and regard. She felt as if their union had shattered an amphora of nectar within her that now flooded her body with sweet exhaustion and relief.

Against her cheek the fierce hammer-strokes of Zack's heart were gradually slowing to a calmer rhythm. Eve felt his lips brush her temple, and then his chest expanded with a deep sigh of satisfaction and contentment. She had sensed that at first he had held himself back, placing her needs above his own, but in the final moments of mindless ecstasy he, too, had been totally claimed by the pagan maelstrom of sexual hedonism. Against her hair he murmured quietly, 'Eve, you truly are the most sensual woman. You were absolutely incredible.'

She lifted her head so that her gaze met his. Her eyes were still bewildered by the force of what she had just experienced with him. Awareness of their surroundings came back slowly, the compact, wood-panelled cabin, the ripples of reflected sunlight off the water that danced over the low ceiling.

'What are you thinking, sweetheart?' Zack asked softly.

She ran her hand over his chest, a catch of emotion in her voice, despite the faint ghost of a laugh as she said, 'I can't believe I've just been seduced on board your cruiser in the middle of the afternoon.'

'Are you shocked?' Zack teased gently.

'A little,' she admitted. 'I've never done anything like this before.'

'I know you haven't, darling,' Zack smiled. 'And believe it or not, I don't make a practice of afternoon seduction.' He raised himself on an elbow and with his other hand smoothed a strand of hair from her face as he said, becoming serious, 'I'm not a womaniser, Eve, not in any way. It's only you I want. I just hope I made it as special for you as you did for me.'

'You did,' she whispered, the initial dazed astonishment that she had let him take her fading against his tender protectiveness in love's afterglow. 'You were so very gentle,' she added softly, tracing a caressing finger along his jaw as she recalled the pleasure he had given and taken.

'I didn't realise you were still a virgin,' he said, his blue eyes searching hers. 'Not at first. Why, Eve? Why didn't you sleep with Simon?'

'I had...' she began, and then faltered.

Zack lifted her wrist to his lips and ran his tongue along the vein. She opened her fingers with the pleasure of it and confessed, 'I had this rather stupidly romantic notion of... of my virginity being a gift to my husband on our wedding-night.'

'It's not stupidly romantic,' Zack smiled. 'It's incredibly sweet.'

'I'm glad now that I waited,' she whispered, blushing prettily, 'that you were the first.'

'I'll be honest with you,' he answered. 'Even if I'd known you were a virgin, it wouldn't have made any difference. I've wanted you naked in my bed ever since that first night, and it was very obvious that you weren't the sort of woman who'd give yourself lightly.'

He broke off and rolled on to his back, amusement tugging attractively at his mouth as he stared up at the ceiling.

'God knows how I'm going to tell you this without *really* sounding like an impossible chauvinist!'

'Tell me what?' she said, answering laughter coming into her voice as she nestled against him.

He pushed her back against the pillows and she felt the full length of his powerful body imprisoning hers. His eyes smiled into hers before he said, his voice suddenly quiet and intense, 'That to make you my wife, I knew I'd have to convince you first that you were my woman. And you are my woman, Eve, mine and only mine.'

Still overwhelmed by the beauty of their lovemaking, Eve felt that marriage was the ultimate way of expressing for ever the harmony of mind and body she now recognised they shared. There were no doubts in her mind, no questions. Her whole body glowed with the radiance of the response he had demanded and elicited from her. The sweet, tender sensation his penetration of her had left was a reminder of the fierce joy of oneness with him.

She slipped her arms up round his neck and kissed him. Immediately he shaped her face with his strong, tanned hands, pressing a series of light kisses along her cheekbone before nibbling her ear.

'Marry me, Eve,' he whispered.

She smiled, too happy to speak.

'Say yes,' he demanded. 'Say yes, you'll marry me.'

And without hesitating she gave him her promise, happy laughter in her voice. 'Yes, Zack, I'll marry you.'

CHAPTER SEVEN

RETURNING to the boatyard, where the usual atmosphere of activity was unaltered, seemed a shade unreal to Eve after the magical interlude on board *Rebel Lady* with Zack. The flag that carried the yard's logo fluttered gently from its pole that rose above the white gables of the chandlery. One of the cruisers in for repair work was being patiently sandblasted by an employee who was muffled in heavy dungarees and face mask. Along the straight stretch of water there was the usual river-traffic.

'It's a shame to have to come back to the real world and break the enchantment,' Eve said, as Zack helped her ashore on to the landing-stage.

'The enchantment's never going to end, my green-eyed witch,' Zack answered, keeping her in the circle of his arm as they strolled towards his car.

They were both reluctant to part. It wasn't until Eve heard Ryan call out to her that she was wanted on the phone that she said reluctantly, 'I'll have to go.'

'What time do you finish work?' Zack asked, his voice caressing her.

'I'll be through by about six. Saturday's always hectic.' Mischief danced in her eyes as she added, 'Especially when you take time out unexpectedly in the afternoon.'

'Honey, the way you turn me on, you're lucky to have got back in time to do any work at all,' Zack growled, making her laugh. 'What time shall I pick you up tonight?'

'Well, I promised I'd visit Dad,' she began.

'OK, I'll call for you at seven and we'll drive up to the hospital and surprise him with the good news. Then afterwards we can go on and have dinner somewhere.'

'Somehow, I don't think Dad's going to be too surprised,' Eve said as she linked her arms round Zack's neck. 'I'm sure he's suspected there's been something going on between us.'

'Well, the sparks certainly flew every time we were together,' Zack answered, amusement in his voice as he bent to kiss her.

It began as a light goodbye kiss, but somehow it deepened and, by the time Zack finally released her, Eve's heart was racing. She remembered suddenly that she was wanted on the phone.

'See you at seven,' she said softly before heading to the chandlery at a run.

The ring Zack bought her was a square-cut emerald, flanked on either side by diamonds. The emerald was so exquisite, enhanced by the dancing fire of the diamonds, that when she slipped it on her finger she was almost dazzled by it.

'It's just beautiful,' she breathed.

'And it's engraved,' Zack said, a familiar teasing note in his voice.

She glanced up at him then slipped the ring off to look inside the gold band. Inside, very small, was engraved the date of the day she had agreed to marry him.

'And you accuse me of being a romantic,' she said with a catch of emotion.

'It's just a reminder of the day you became my woman,' he said, provoking her to laughter as he drew her into his arms.

The official announcement of their engagement appeared in *The Times* the following week, though they hadn't yet set a date for the wedding. With her father ill, Eve didn't feel she could make plans till the results of his tests were known. Zack was understanding, though he made it clear that he wanted the wedding to take place soon.

At times she wondered if she was crazy, committing herself to a man she'd known no more than a matter of weeks. But if she was, she knew she never wanted to be sane again. She was more deeply in love than she'd ever been in her life. Both physically and mentally, she seemed to have been made to mesh with Zack.

The decision as to where they should live after they were married they made easily. While Zack had a prestige flat fronting on to the water at Marlow for weekend use, his permanent base was on Harrow Hill. Eve could easily drive from there to the boatyard each day on the M4, and immediately she saw the house she knew she wanted to live there.

It was modern, with a lovely feeling of space and light. The patio doors in the large living-room gave a sweeping view over the lower slopes of the hill with the farm and playing-fields of Harrow School, while beyond was the built-up area of London.

'On a very clear day,' Zack told her as he came and stood beside her, slipping an arm round her waist, 'you can pick out the Post Office Tower from here.'

'It's lovely,' she said as, arms linked, they strolled into the garden and down the shallow steps that led from the patio to the lawns. 'Did you have the garden profession-ally landscaped?'

'A friend of mine who does landscaping helped draw up the plans, and a gardener looks in once a week,' Zack told her. 'Occasionally I do a bit myself when I get the time.'

A sole apple tree, old and gnarled, obviously left when the house was built, spread its thick branches over the lower lawns. Seeing the home-made swing which hung on it, Eve queried teasingly, 'Is this where you spend your time gardening?'

'It's for my sister's kids,' Zack laughed. 'You'll meet her two little girls this weekend. Suzanne and James have asked us for dinner on Saturday.'

'Where do they live?' Eve asked as she sat down on the swing. She glanced up at Zack and added playfully, 'I don't seem to know very much about you.'

Zack nuzzled her neck wickedly and said in a low voice, 'I thought we knew each other most intimately.'

Giggling, she tried to fend him off. He let her, and then gave the swing a series of strong pushes.

'My sister lives just outside Oxford,' he told her as he sent her soaring up. 'James is a reader at the university and, as for knowing more about me, we've a lifetime of discovery ahead of us.'

'That's enough!' she laughed helplessly as her skirt billowed out above her knees and her dark hair flew about her face. 'Please Zack, not any higher!'

'You're quite safe. Just don't let go,' he teased, giving her one more push before catching the swing and pulling her into his arms. He kissed her and said, 'Do you know how much you reminded me of Fragonard's painting, "La Balançoire" just now?'

'I hope I didn't show quite as much petticoat as the artist's model!'

'That's part of the painting's charm. Besides, I'm sure you're far more modestly dressed than she was.'

'What do you mean?' Eve asked, suspiciously, amusement dancing in her eyes.

'Well, the girl in the painting may have been wearing a petticoat, but that was the full extent of her lingerie. Why do you think her lover's gazing up and looking so mesmerised in the foreground?'

'You're having me on,' Eve laughed protestingly. 'I don't believe it. Anyway, how do you know?'

'A short history of art course I went on once. Didn't you know? The painting used to be regarded as wickedly erotic. It's only recently that it's become respectable.'

'Which is more than you'll ever be,' Eve teased.

She had never met anyone before who was such good company. Whoever had said that a sense of humour was one of the sexiest attributes a man could have had been absolutely right. They strolled back towards the house, crossed the balustraded patio and went into the lounge.

'If there's anything about the house you don't like,' Zack said easily, 'change it.' Then, seeing she was about to protest that there was nothing she wanted to alter, he added, 'I mean it. It's going to be your home, Eve. You can have it exactly as you want.'

'You're very good to me,' she said softly.

'So I should be,' he smiled. 'You've given me so much. More than you know.'

She smiled back before slipping gently out of his embrace to look at the room in more detail. There was a Steinway piano in one corner and she walked towards it. She knew Zack enjoyed classical music, particularly Chopin, and she commented, 'I didn't know you played.'

Zack didn't answer, and immediately Eve sensed that there was something taut in the brief silence. She glanced back at him, her eyes questioning. Zack's expression was remote and unreadable.

'It was my wife, Jocelyn, who used to play,' he said almost curtly, before asking, 'Do you want to see the upstairs?'

It was one of the few times he'd mentioned his first marriage. Eve knew he and Jocelyn had not had children because, after a miscarriage, becoming pregnant again had been too great a risk to Jocelyn's health. Apart from the brief facts of how long he'd been married, that was all Zack had told her. She hadn't thought to ask more. Everything that there was between her and Zack pointed to the fact that she had no need to ask, no need to feel the slightest stab of insecure jealousy of Jocelyn—until this moment.

'Yes, I'd like to see the rest of the house,' she said, very conscious of a sudden barrier between them.

Since that afternoon on board *Rebel Lady*, she'd felt there was nothing she couldn't say to him, but now she was deliberately checking a torrent of questions she wanted to ask him about his dead wife. She followed him upstairs, no longer thinking of how much she was looking forward to living here with him, but wondering suddenly if he had shared this house with Jocelyn. Why ever hadn't such a fundamental question occurred to her before? Trying to sound casual, she asked, 'How long have you lived here?'

'About two years.'

And he'd been widowed for just over a year. So this had been Jocelyn's home, she thought with a stab of dismay.

Zack took her hand as he led her along the galleried landing, opening doors as they came to them.

'There are three visitors' rooms,' he told her, before adding speculatively, his blue eyes teasing her affectionately, 'or... children's rooms?'

'Three?' she queried as the unease of a moment ago suddenly ebbed.

She was being ridiculously over-sensitive. What did it matter that he had lived here with Jocelyn in the last year of their marriage? After all, hadn't he said she could change anything in the house she wanted? He wouldn't have said that if he wasn't over his wife's death. Jocelyn was part of his past in the same way that Simon was part of hers. But it didn't mean she needed to be jealous.

'Well, maybe not three.' Zack's smile was attractively knowing. He drew her into his arms, kissing her lightly on the lips before saying softly, 'How about two? Both with laughing green eyes like their mother.'

She blushed a little, but there was agreement in the glance that flashed between them, before he led her into the master bedroom. Zack slid his hands into the pockets of his jeans while Eve wandered into the centre of the room and looked around her.

'I know you'll want to add some feminine touches to it,' he commented. 'It's a bit Spartan.'

She moved towards the french windows, seeing the white wrought-iron balcony and the blue-tinged evening view beyond. If this was the room he had once shared with his wife, he must have altered it radically since her death. There was a TV in one corner and there were a number of books on the table to the side of the double bed. But there were no ornaments, few softening touches, and beige was the predominant colour. On the walls were two enigmatic pictures of clowns, with a melancholy about them which only came out when they were studied more closely. As she stood in front of them, Zack joined her and lifted one of them down.

'I think I've looked at these long enough,' he commented. 'One of your riverscapes would be a vast improvement.'

'That's good, because I'm planning on giving you that picture I wouldn't let you buy, as a wedding present.'

'I'll treasure it,' he said, kissing her temple.

'Can I really have a free hand with this room?' she asked.

'Anything you want,' Zack agreed. 'Redecorations, new furniture, the lot, just so long as you make it nice and feminine. I like the clutter a woman leaves about a house. I want to see your scent bottles and jewellery on the dressing-table and your stockings thrown on the bed. I'll even put up with fine dusting talc over everything.'

He slid his hands down her arms in a caress before pulling her close.

'I'm not *that* untidy,' she joked as she imagined her belongings in the room, *their* room.

Almost inadvertently her eyes went to the large double bed, and Zack asked devilishly, 'Are you thinking what I hope you're thinking?'

It had been a warm day, and she was wearing a crinkle-cotton sun-dress. Deftly Zack slipped one of the shoulder straps down her arm, his hand caressing her smooth skin. No man had ever touched her with such erotically knowing hands, and she breathed huskily, 'I can't think at all when you do that!'

He laughed softly, and then very gently and sensuously bit her earlobe.

'Zack!' she gasped, her heart racing.

'Do you want me to stop?' he murmured teasingly.

'No,' she whispered with intensity, pleasure pulsing through her at his tantalising seduction of her senses.

For a while there was only the sound of her quickened breathing as Zack rained kisses down her throat. She arched her neck for him. Then, feverishly, her fingers tugged his shirt undone so she could run her hands with an ardent need over the width of his chest, savouring the hard-muscled strength of him.

'God, Eve, you drive me crazy,' he groaned as he swept her off her feet and lowered her onto the large double bed.

And then reality and time were lost in the drowning sweet turbulence of their lovemaking.

The radiance Eve had found in her relationship with Zack seemed to pour into every channel of her life. She had never coped with the minor hassles of work with so much ease or with such confidence.

The next morning at work the usual series of problems cropped up. One of the engineers showed up late for work, a cruiser came back damaged, its propellor entangled with an old mattress someone had dumped in the river, and the Calor Gas delivery failed to arrive. Eve was about to contact their suppliers when Jill came into her office.

'Have you got a minute, Eve?' she began.

'Yes, of course. What's the problem?'

'We have had so many towels walk off the boats this season, we're going to have to order some more,' Jill complained. 'It's a good job we ask for a deposit on the linen.'

'Tell me what we need and I'll get the order off first thing next week.'

Jill grumbled some more about the thoughtlessness of people and then smiled and said, 'I suppose when you've just got engaged to a man like Zack Thole, missing towels seem trivial.'

Eve laughed and then reached out a finger to touch one of the carnations in the arrangement on her desk, her eyes soft.

'Right now,' she admitted as she came back to the present, 'the only real worry I've got is Dad.'

'How much longer will he have to stay in hospital?'

'I don't know. In fact, I've been wondering if I ought to get in touch with Robin and tell him what's happening. He'll be back from his holiday in just over a week, but all the same, *if* anything's wrong, he'll say I should have contacted him.'

'The tests still haven't shown up anything?' Jill queried.

'The only thing that's been established definitely is that Dad isn't suffering from heart-trouble.'

'I'm sure he'll be OK,' Jill said. She dropped a sympathetic hand on Eve's shoulder as she added, 'Anyway, I must get back to checking the laundry. See you later.'

She went out, and Eve stood up and crossed over to the filing cabinet in the corner. She had her back to the door when she heard it open. Thinking that Jill had forgotten something she glanced round, but instead Greg came into her office with an enormous bunch of red roses.

'You see,' he announced as he presented them to her with a slight flourish. 'This time I didn't forget the lady likes flowers.'

She took them from him and put them down on top of the photocopier, saying with a mixture of surprise and coolness, 'What are you doing here?'

Greg came and perched on the corner of her desk. He looked down an instant to study his hands. Then he glanced back at her and said, the banter stripped from his tone, 'You *know* why I'm here. I've missed you. I should never have left things between us the way I did before I went to New York. Eve, I've been a fool. I've done nothing but think about you the whole time I've been away. I don't know what came over me when I walked out on you at the pub that night. I don't blame you if you're still angry with me.'

'I'm not...' she began.

'Then let's start again,' he cut across her, getting up from the desk and taking hold of her by the shoulders.

'We can't,' she said, moving away. 'Greg, things are over between us.'

'Because I lost my temper and left you stranded at the pub?' he asked, sounding angry, rather than apologetic.

'No, because...' She paused and then said more gently, 'Greg, I'm sorry, because I know this is going to come as a shock to you, but I'm engaged to be married.'

There was a moment's stunned silence. Then Greg exclaimed with a short, incredulous laugh, 'You're not serious!'

'I'm perfectly serious.'

He snatched hold of her left hand and then, seeing the emerald ring that confirmed what she'd told him, he let go of it, his dark eyes glinting.

'My God!' he exploded in a low voice vibrant with fury. 'In over a year I get all of nowhere with you. I don't even get you into bed, and in the space of a fortnight, while I'm away in New York, you get engaged to another man. Well, who is he, Eve? Who's the lucky man who cleans up the moment I'm off the scene?'

'Greg, stop it,' she said sharply. 'You knew it was over between us before you went away.'

He grabbed hold of her by the shoulders and started to shake her.

'*Who* is he?' he demanded.

She thumped her fist against his chest and broke free. Clearing her hair back from her forehead with a sweeping movement of her hand, she conceded angrily, 'All right. It's Zack. Zack Thole. And now I want you to leave.'

Greg stared at her with a fixity that gave a driving malevolence to his saturnine face. Then he turned towards her desk and crashed his fist down on it.

'God!' he exclaimed savagely. 'Hasn't he done enough without this?' He swung back towards her, snatching hold of her arm as he breathed furiously, 'You stupid little bitch, don't you realise what he's doing?'

'Let go of me!' she demanded. 'You're behaving like a madman.'

'Madman? No, I'm not the madman. The person who's crazy is that bastard who's hounded me ever since I broke up his marriage.'

There was an instant's incredulous silence and then Eve breathed, 'What... what did you say?'

'No, Zack didn't tell you that, did he?' Greg sneered with harsh sarcasm. 'You didn't know that his wife ran off with me...'

'I don't want to hear about this,' she cut him short.

'You don't really think Zack's in love with you, do you?' Greg ploughed on savagely. 'Because, let me tell you, he's not interested in *you*. All he cares about is the fact that you're mine.'

'I'm not yours and this is absurd,' she said, her voice becoming shrill.

'Absurd?' Greg laughed harshly. 'God, yes, you'd think so. You'd think by now, Zack would bury the past.'

'I won't listen to any more,' she said angrily. 'You're a poor loser, Greg, and you're just being hateful. I love Zack and I won't hear a word against him.'

'Well, maybe it's time you thought about what his feelings for you are. Because you're a goddamn fool if you think he loves you. It was Jocelyn he loved. He was crazy about her. If she'd asked for the moon he'd have got it for her. He wouldn't even let her try for another baby after she lost their first, he was so protective of her. He was so possessive he hardly let her out of his sight...'

'Shut up,' she insisted.

For an answer he grabbed hold of her arm, continuing as if she'd never interrupted, 'And then Jocelyn left him for me. And maybe he'd have got over the fact that I took her away from and that I slept with her. But instead there was that accident, the accident he blames me for, and swore I'd pay for.'

'I don't believe a word of this,' Eve whispered, her face drained of colour.

'Don't you?' Greg said, his eyes full of rage. 'What version of the story has he given you?' Eve didn't answer and he swept on, 'He hasn't told you anything about it at all, has he?'

'Zack *loves* me,' she said, her voice cramped with vehemence and emotion.

'And I'll tell you when that love started,' Greg answered. 'The moment he knew you were involved with me. Because this is his final way of getting revenge, of making me pay for the fact that Jocelyn's dead. I took his woman, and so now he's taking mine.'

Eve stared at him with tormented eyes, her throat stranglingly tight. She wanted to scream at Greg that every word he had said was all lies. It couldn't be true. She couldn't stand it if it were. Pain slashed at her heart and she stormed, her voice no longer under control, 'Get out of here!'

'Finish with him, Eve,' Greg ordered.

She flung her arm out towards the door and advanced towards him, a slim fury. 'Get out before I have you thrown out! And don't you ever set foot in here again.'

'You won't see the truth even when it's staring you in the face. Well, all right, be a gullible fool and put us both in hell, because if I've lost you, it's to a man who only wants you for his revenge.'

He went out, slamming the door behind him. Immediately Eve dropped shakily into the chair behind her desk. Leaning her elbows on it, she covered her face with her hands. The agony and shock went too deep for tears. She felt she couldn't stand the knife of pain that tore at her heart. She looked up at the vase of carnations on her desk and with an angry sweep of her hand knocked it on the floor. The destruction stemmed for an instant the agony of heartbreak. Furiously she snatched up the pen-holder on her desk and sent that smashing on to the floor as well.

And then, suddenly, her shoulders began to shake. She clenched her hands in her determination not to give way to a storm of tempestuous tears. She'd sworn after

Simon that she'd never cry over a man again. But to be betrayed twice!

She looked at her emerald ring, about to snatch it off, when she remembered the engraving inside it, the endearments Zack had said to her, the way he had made love to her. It couldn't be true that he was only using her as an instrument of revenge. The telephone on her desk started ringing. She stared at it for an instant before walking abruptly out of her office, grabbing her jacket and bag as she went. She had to get away.

Ryan was at the chandlery counter serving a customer. She interrupted him to say tautly, 'Deal with any calls for me, will you, Ryan? I'm going out.'

Her car was parked on the stretch of sun-brightened concrete outside. She switched on the engine and pulled away with a roar of acceleration. To be at the wheel calmed her a little. Vehemently she tried to refute what Greg had told her. She refused to believe it, any of it. Yet fragments of the past few weeks kept flashing relentlessly through her mind as she drove. She thought of the flowers Zack had sent her every day, the single-mindedness with which he'd pursued and seduced her.

The signpost ahead reminded her that she was approaching the main road into London. She'd been driving with no idea of where she was heading. Now she remembered she had told her father she'd visit him that afternoon. Suddenly she felt desperate for the comfort of being with someone whose love was completely certain.

The traffic was heavy as she neared London, and she drove aggressively, ready to blow impatiently at the least bit of incompetent driving. The misery had settled down now to a pain as nagging as grief.

As she parked her car and walked into the hospital, she thought suddenly of Zack's reaction when she had asked him if he played the piano. She'd sensed then that something was wrong, that he wasn't over Jocelyn's death, that his dead wife was a barrier between them. Why hadn't she listened to her feelings? Why hadn't she wondered why he scarcely mentioned Jocelyn? She must have been blind not to have realised that the reason he didn't talk about her was that he couldn't bear to be reminded.

She paused for a second outside the door to her father's room. The nurse on duty had said she could go straight in, but Eve needed a moment to steady herself. She didn't want her father to see how distraught she was, not now when he was ill. Summoning up what she could of a pretence of brightness, she went into the room.

Frank was sitting in an armchair by the bed, tackling the *Telegraph* crossword. Her heart contracted a little at seeing him. It was a long time since he'd been able to fix whatever was wrong for her, as he'd seemed to when she was small. But somehow, even now, just being with him made the tearing uncertainty about Zack's love easier to bear.

Frank put the paper aside and took off his glasses.

'Eve,' he said delightedly, 'how nice to see you! I rang the boatyard about an hour ago, but Ryan said you'd already left.'

'I thought I'd visit you early today,' she said as she sat down. 'How are you feeling?'

'That's why I tried to phone you. I've had the results of the tests today and there's nothing seriously wrong. It turns out that what's been causing the dizzy spells I've been getting is mild diabetes. The doctor tells me diet alone should put things right, and I'm being discharged tomorrow.'

'Oh, Dad,' Eve exclaimed, her voice unsteady, 'that's wonderful news!'

Relief, coupled with emotional stress, made her courage break abruptly. She found she was crying, and to her consternation she couldn't stop the tears. Frank took hold of her hand and began to pat it.

'Eve, darling,' he began in concern. 'Pet, you mustn't cry. Everything's all right.'

'I know,' she gulped, fumbling for a handkerchief and wiping her eyes fiercely. 'It's just such a relief... and I'm... b-being stupid.'

'Of course you're not,' Frank said comfortingly. 'It's been a worrying time. But things will be back to normal again now. I'm even hoping to go into the boatyard on Saturday.'

If he said that now she'd have more time at the weekend to spend with Zack, she knew she'd start crying again. Quickly she said, struggling to keep her voice steady, 'I think we're going to have to change our suppliers of Calor Gas. The delivery didn't arrive today, and I haven't got round yet to chasing it up.'

The diversion tactic worked. The business was Frank's life, and, having been away from the boatyard for a week, he was only too ready to make it the main topic of conversation. They talked for a while before there was a tap at the door. One of the nurses bustled in to say the dietitian was on her way up to advise Frank how best to keep his diabetes under control.

'Eve,' Frank said thoughtfully as she stood up to go. 'When you get back to the yard, get straight on to Salter's and find out about their charges for Calor Gas. If they can come up with a competitive price, we'll change suppliers.'

'OK, I'll do that,' she agreed, not admitting that she'd intended to call it a day at work.

She left the hospital, walking briskly, her shoulders squared, despite the numbness she felt inside. She got into her Maestro. The sunlight through the car window made the diamonds on her left hand as she held the wheel flash rainbow colours.

The dancing brilliance seemed to mock her. Greg had told her of the bitter rivalry that had always existed between him and Zack. If it existed in business, then how much more so over a woman? For all her efforts, she couldn't stop the mustard seed of doubt growing. She remembered the flowers Zack had sent her, the way he'd taken advantage of her vulnerability on board his cruiser. Naïve romantic that she'd been, she'd believed in him. Now she saw too late that of course his pursuit of her had been too single-minded, their courtship too quick. It hadn't been motivated by love at all. Zack's motive had been his obsession for revenge. He was marrying her solely to equal the account with Greg over Jocelyn.

And in that moment she knew she wasn't driving back to the boatyard. She couldn't deceive herself any longer. What Greg had told her was the truth. Everything he'd said fitted so neatly with the facts. She clamped down on the memory of the way Zack had made love to her, because the sharp uprise of pain was more than she could stand.

She knew his office was in Holborn. And she was going there to hand him back his ring and tell him she wouldn't marry him.

CHAPTER EIGHT

EVE swung her car on to the main road. What a credulous fool she had been, she thought angrily, to believe Zack was in love with her. Deborah had even told her that night at the party that no one could take his dead wife's place for him. Why hadn't she taken note of that? What exactly had she thought was so special about her that a dynamic, hard-headed man like Zack Thole, who could have just about any woman he wanted, should have proposed marriage to her when they hadn't known each other more than a few weeks?

But he hadn't had to use her as an instrument of vengeance. Hatred of him flared up as intense as her love for him had been. She thought of the sense of completeness she had discovered with him, a completeness she had never known before, and the anguish was worse than any physical pain. What she was going to do was to fling his emerald ring back at him, but nothing, nothing could dull the feeling of being torn asunder, of being less than whole.

She left her car on a meter, though she was in such a mood of reckless anger she would have taken a risk on a double yellow line. She stormed through the double doors of the tall office block with its imposing frontage.

The security officer at the desk asked her name and then indicated the lift. It glided up and then opened on to an expanse of carpeted foyer. Eve stepped out. The atmosphere of serene efficiency was pervasive. It steadied her. Suddenly she knew that, whatever her feelings were, she wasn't going to let Zack see how devastated she was.

She remembered the faint contempt she had seen in his blue eyes when he had learned that she was Greg's girlfriend. She wasn't going to have that dismissive contempt deepen by creating a scene here at his company headquarters. When she told him she wasn't going to marry him, she was going to be as cold and as hard and as unmoving as he had apparently been in his seduction of her.

Deborah pushed through the swing doors and came towards her.

'Hello, Eve,' she began brightly. 'This is a nice surprise. I haven't had a chance yet to congratulate you on your engagement. I'm afraid Zack's in a meeting at the moment, but I'm sure he won't mind my interrupting it to tell him that you're here.'

'No, don't do that,' Eve said quickly. 'I'd rather leave a message.'

'OK, if you're sure,' Deborah agreed. 'I'll show you into his office.'

Still chatting, Deborah led the way. Eve was silent. She was thinking that Deborah wouldn't be the only friend she'd eventually have to tell she had broken off her engagement.

Well, for now, she'd leave the explaining to Zack. After all, why not, when it was his double dealing that meant everything was over between them? Undoubtedly he would come up with some plausible explanation when he told Deborah the news. When it came to calculating deviousness, he was the expert.

'Would you like coffee?' Deborah asked as she let Eve precede her into an outer office.

Eve noticed its elegant décor, and the display of foliage plants on Deborah's desk, the comfortable leather sofas and chairs with a low table scattered with marketing magazines placed in the middle.

'Thanks, but no,' she answered, her voice a shade tight. 'I'm in a hurry this afternoon.'

Deborah showed her into Zack's office and Eve paused for an instant just inside the door. It was just as she would have expected. There was a personal computer on the leather-topped desk that showed a heavy but well-organised workload. His office was prestigious but functional, its aura of the fast-moving, modern business world so strongly evocative of the man himself that she was desperate to get away.

Briskly she went up to his desk. Setting her bag down, she drew a piece of headed paper towards her. She wrote the first words that came into her mind.

'Zack, I find I can't marry you, so I'm returning your ring.'

She paused and then realised wretchedly that there was, after all, nothing more to add. Brushing a hand across her cheek before a tear could fall on the paper, she signed her name. She dropped the ring into an envelope with the note and left it prominently placed on top of his desk diary.

She went back into Deborah's office to see her talking to Stephanie. Eve's heart plummeted. Fencing with Stephanie's subtle form of bitching was more than she could handle at this moment.

'Leave the reports with me, Stephanie, and I'll see Zack gets them,' Deborah said.

Stephanie didn't answer her. She slipped her hands into the pockets of her couture dress and strolled towards Eve.

'So you're going to be the new Mrs Thole,' she began with icy sweetness. 'Well, it's certainly been a whirlwind courtship. How did you manage it?'

'Just the usual feminine mystique,' Eve answered. 'I'm sorry, Deborah, I must rush,' she continued, knowing that if she didn't escape this minute her composure would snap. 'I want to be back at the boatyard before five.'

She felt Stephanie's cold gaze follow her out. Stephanie had obviously hoped that Zack would marry her once he was over Jocelyn's death. Well, she didn't know the half of it, though undoubtedly she'd receive the news that there was to be no wedding with sheer jubilation. And doubtless, too, she'd know how to offer consolation, Eve thought, and then tried to lose the idea because the jealousy was more than she could stand.

Ryan was surprised to see her when she drove into the yard so near to closing time. He was helping a customer to get paint aboard. He crossed over to speak to her.

'How's Frank?' he asked, and she knew from the concern in his voice that she must look more shaken than she'd thought.

'He's fine,' she said quickly. 'In fact, he hopes to be back at work on Saturday.'

'Well now, that's wonderful news!' Ryan exclaimed, genuinely pleased.

Eve smiled and said, 'I've got a few things to sort out for Dad in his office before I go home. If any personal calls come through on my phone, say I'm busy.'

'Sure,' Ryan agreed.

She knew it was more than highly probable that Zack would call her. And when he did, she had nothing to say to him. There was no explanation she intended to give him for her change of mind. Greg had told her Zack had set her up for his own private vendetta, but he was never going to suspect that she'd found out. He could think she'd broken off their engagement for reasons of her own, because he was never having any sense of satisfaction from knowing how shattered she was by this, her second betrayal by a man. This time she was hiding her emotions behind a defensive wall that a lifetime of battering couldn't breach.

Hatred and anger were the best antidotes to the deep, wrenching pain she felt. Damn Zack, she thought furiously. If only she could strike back at him, make him feel something of the wretchedness that was engulfing her. Yes, she was sorry for him that he'd lost his wife. Strangely, it even hurt her to think he could have suffered so much. What she couldn't forgive, what she would always hate him for, was his treating her like some kind of pawn whose feelings and emotions were of no consequence so long as, through her, he could get even with Greg. She remembered how he had called her his woman. Greg had used the same term. That was all she was—a possession in a power game of revenge between two men.

But this time she'd learned her lesson! No man would ever get within emotional reach of her again. She hated and mistrusted the whole sex.

To convince herself that she could deal with even this private disaster, she worked late. Still testing herself, she went back to her office to clear up the broken glass from the vase she had smashed in her anger and despair that morning. The petals of pink carnations that lay on the floor had turned brown in the heat and were dying. They seemed symbolic.

The yard was quiet and completely deserted by the time she was ready to go home. She locked the door to the chandlery and was walking slowly towards her car when Zack's Jaguar swung in at speed through the yard's gates. Her immediate instinct was to run. Except there was no time even for an attempt at flight. Zack stopped the car dead and leapt out, forcefulness lending a pagan energy to his movements. Snatching hold of her wrist, he walked her to the passenger-door.

'Get in,' he ordered brusquely.

'I will not,' she retaliated, recovered enough now to put up a spirited show of resistance. 'I'm going home.'

'Not yet, you're not.'

Zack forced her into the car and then got in alongside her.

'Now, you listen to me,' she rounded on him, her voice rising sharply, as he reversed the car and pulled out through the boatyard gates at some speed. 'I will *not* be treated in this high-handed way. You damn well stop this car. Right now, do you hear? Because I'm getting out and going home.'

Zack's face was set hard.

'Not until we've talked,' he said, his voice grimly calm. 'And after that curt one-line note you left in my office this afternoon, believe me, we've got plenty to talk about.'

He stabbed a glance at her, and the dangerous glitter she saw in his eyes jolted her into silence. She realised suddenly that he was furious with her, but not with the quick, flaring anger that would have told her that he did love her after all, that Greg had been lying. Instead, his anger was controlled and cumulative, the remorseless anger of a man capable of dedicating himself to vengeance.

'I don't have to give you one word of explanation,' she flared as she struggled against tears. 'I'm not marrying you, Zack. And that's all you need to know.'

'We'll argue about that in a minute,' Zack said evenly, his profile hawkish and stern as he kept his eyes intently on the road.

She knew she couldn't trust her voice to answer. The atmosphere vibrated like a wire as Zack drove the short distance to his *pied-á-terre* that was near Marlow Weir. In the silence Eve's resentment against him stiffened, making her more in control of her emotions, so that by the time he pulled into the quiet close she was a simmering hostile fury.

'I'm not coming into your flat with you,' she ground out as Zack opened the car door for her.

He caught hold of her by the arm and pulled her out of the car, not roughly, but with a ruthless implacability that didn't tolerate resistance. There was no semblance of rapport between them now. Zack was a menacing stranger, not the lover she had laughed with and given herself to. His grip was like a vice as he marshalled her inside.

She had never expected that her first visit to his river-front flat would be made under duress. She had time to form only the most superficial impression of the large sitting-room with its picture-window view of the tumbling weir and its clean-cut, expensive furniture. The warm evening sunlight that flooded the room in no way diminished the throbbing tension between them.

'OK,' Zack began with ominous restraint, his blue eyes brutally hard as they stabbed hers. 'What did Stephanie say to you this afternoon?'

'What could she have said to me?' Eve flashed back.

'Well, at a guess, she mentioned my wife,' Zack replied with dry cynicism.

'Jocelyn?' Eve said shrilly. 'What do you imagine Stephanie said about her? Because whatever she'd told me, it would be more than you have, wouldn't it? Well, no,' she rushed on, 'as a matter of fact Stephanie didn't say anything to me...'

Zack pulled her towards him firmly and she said, her voice rising, 'I'm not marrying you. And what's more, I never damn well intended to.'

It was an empty, defiant statement, prompted by her desire to find a way somehow to hurt him in return for the anguish he was causing her.

'You'd better explain that,' Zack said, force behind his words.

'It's Greg I love,' she said vehemently, 'not you. I saw him this afternoon...'

'Are you telling me you've been playing me off against him?'

His fingers had tightened painfully on her arm, but she was too distraught to heed it. Instead, seizing the idea he had given her, she said, forcing the words out and hating the way she sounded, 'I thought I'd never get Greg to marry me without some kind of spur. He's not the first man who's needed a rival to bring him to the boil.'

Zack let her go so suddenly that she staggered a little.

'You told me you'd split up with Greg,' he said, his voice level despite the glint of restrained anger in his eyes.

It should have warned her that she was going too far, but she wasn't in any state to be rational. And in any case, she was far more afraid of his razor-sharp mind than his temper, of his judgement that wasn't clouded by emotion. It was so blatantly obvious now that he didn't love her. But he was never going to have the triumph of knowing how deeply she'd loved him.

His questioning of her had the cold, driving precision of a lawyer, none of the raw, mounting anger of a jealous lover. His indifference to her made a suffocating hatred of him engulf her, consuming her with a need to hurt him as he'd hurt her. Venomously she began, 'I said I wouldn't sleep with Greg. I wanted to be his wife, not his mistress. He was taking me for granted and I wanted to make him jealous...'

'You'd better not be saying what I think you are,' Zack cut across her with concentrated anger.

Exultant at the thought that she had got back at him if only a little, she demanded derisively, 'Why? Does it hurt your male pride to think I was only using you as a rival?'

'Are you telling me you've broken off our engagement because Greg's asked you to marry him?' Zack said, snatching hold of her with swift violence.

'I love him,' she lied with all the sharp vehemence of pain.

She gasped and broke off as Zack shook her, suddenly making her hair tumble across her face.

'Love him!' he repeated. 'You stupid little fool! You don't even match up with him enough physically to have slept with him.'

'Stop it,' she sobbed. 'I hate you.'

For an instant Zack held her rigid, his blue eyes ablaze as they stared down at her, the line of his cheekbones ruthless. With an effort he mastered his temper and said with visible restraint, 'Eve, make sense. If you're not in love with me, why did you let me seduce you that day? Why have you been sleeping with me since?'

The heart-wrenching pain she felt at the reminder of their lovemaking was so intense that she thought she'd break down in tears. Before she knew what she was doing, she slapped him across the face.

She expected him to let go of her. Instead, with a blaze of rage in his eyes, he crushed her to him. Ineffectually she beat a hand against his shoulder, but she was arched backwards by his arm that encircled her waist.

'No!' she gasped.

'Does Greg make you feel the way I do?' he demanded.

'I don't feel anything for you at all!'

'Then let me prove you wrong,' he muttered.

Raking a hand through her hair, he bent his head to kiss her. His lips were insistent and demanding as he enveloped her in his embrace, stirring in her an excitement she tried to suppress. She made a soft moan in her throat as Zack's kiss became more intimate, seeming to promise a passionate tenderness she knew to be a lie. He held her possessively and, dizzy and breathless, she stopped her feeble struggles, unable to fight any longer her need to kiss him back.

When he finally raised his head she was trembling, her eyes dark and wide in her pale face. She felt so weak, she thought she would faint.

'Now tell me you don't love me,' Zack muttered fiercely.

'Leave me alone,' she whispered shakenly.

'What are you afraid of, Eve? Your feelings? Are you backing out of marrying me because you're scared of your own emotions? You don't belong to Greg...'

'Because I'm *your* woman?' she flared with renewed defiance. 'Well, I'm not. And just because I was crazy enough to go to bed with you doesn't make me yours. Do you understand? I belong to myself and no one else, and when I sleep with Greg he won't own me either!'

'I won't let you sleep with Greg,' he warned.

'You can't stop me from doing a damned thing,' she retaliated.

For an answer, Zack lifted her off her feet and strode with her into his bedroom.

'What the hell do you think you're doing?' she demanded, striking a furious hand against his shoulder.

'You belong to me, Eve, and you're going to admit it,' he said harshly as he dropped her on to the bed.

She tried to slither off it, but he was too quick for her. Imprisoning her with his body, his mouth descended on hers in another ravishing, soul-searching kiss. There was no escape from his strong arms, and in any case her senses were already beginning to welcome his driving passion. A shock of pleasure went through her and she realised his hand was caressing the warm softness of her breast. With a mixture of panic and fury she thumped against his arm, her breathing so ragged she could hardly speak.

'You b-brute. I hate you.'

He caught hold of both her hands, towering over her as his blue eyes blazed into hers.

'Hate? No, Eve, I don't think so.'

'You're n-not getting even with Greg by raping me!' she said in a choked voice.

'Rape!' Zack said harshly. 'You call it rape when you kiss me the way you do?'

Colour flamed in her face as she sobbed, 'Let me up.'

'Let you escape? Never, Eve.'

He bent his head slowly to kiss the hollow of her throat. Then his hands slid fluently beneath her blouse, his strong, experienced fingers caressing her as though he was mesmerised by the feel of her. Tears stung her closed eyes as she tried to suppress the shudder of helpless wanting that went through her.

She was about to plead with him to stop as his mouth found hers again, demanding and devouring while his fingers stroked her waist with the gentleness with which he had always made love to her. How could he touch her like this when he felt nothing for her? Or was he such an experienced lover that seduction for him was simply a practised art? Anguish fought with the feverish ache of desire and, as he slid her blouse from her shoulders, in desperate panic she sank her teeth into his wrist.

He swore under his breath and wrenched her skirt from her.

'Don't!' she cried. 'Please, don't do this to me.'

'Then tell me you don't want me,' he said raggedly as he kissed her breasts.

A shudder went through her, stifling the words so that all she managed was to whisper his name. His shirt was open and she could see the harsh rise and fall of his deep chest. She tried to twist from underneath him, but his arms came round her, moulding her softness to him.

'Don't fight me, Eve,' he breathed. 'You know you want me.'

Her moan of desperation mirrored her drowning need to give herself up to his tormentingly gentle yet powerful lovemaking. Against her will her clenched hands opened and she traced them upwards over his chest, feeling his ribs corrugated beneath his hair-roughened skin. She trembled as he caressed her, scarcely able to breathe, her heart clamouring with wild beats.

His mouth closed over her taut nipple and she gave a gasping moan as pleasure pierced her. Her dazed mind tried to hold on to the fact that he was seducing her solely out of a determination to cheat Greg out of marrying her, to get his revenge. But reason faltered and was then lost, erased by the driving, primitive hunger he was arousing in her. Excited by his touch, she was as elemental as time, a primeval woman, the first Eve. Her skin felt on fire from his hungry kisses and erotic messenger hands.

She could no longer stifle the husky pleas she made for him to free her from the dark, swirling pleasure that was engulfing her. A pagan enchantment made her respond to him with a wildness she could no longer contain. He was taking her to ever greater heights and she clutched at his shoulders, delirious with the need to be united with him. And then, as the peak of pleasure became more than she could bear, Zack came over and into her. She could sense his possessive triumph at her abandon, but she was too far lost in the mists of obscuring pleasure to do anything but welcome him, too overpowered by the helpless waves that were showering her body with delight.

When it was over, she lay bewildered, her heart still beating heavily, a sensual satedness making her stay unmoving, her hands uncurled and relaxed after the ecstasy of climax. Zack moved from her, and the shift of his weight made sudden realisation of what had happened rush over her. Suppressing a sob, she turned away from him, pressing her hot face into the pillow. He had made love to her with a heady, demanding passion, yet she felt violated in both body and spirit, her self-respect in ruins after her complete submission to him.

Defiance hid the shine of tears in her eyes as Zack put a hand on her shoulder.

'Don't touch me!' she breathed, flinching.

The gentleness went out of his fingers as he turned her back imperatively to face him.

'That's a strange thing to say after the way you've just responded to me. I'd no idea you could be such a wild little temptress.'

She turned her head away, swallowing against the strangling tightness in her throat. There would be time enough to torment herself with memories of this room and this bed in the days ahead.

'You've had all the revenge you're getting through me,' she whispered harshly.

'What exactly are you accusing me of?' he demanded, sliding his hand over her waist.

Resisting him, she gasped in panic as she felt the intimacy of his naked body.

'I said don't touch me! Now get up and get out of here so I can get dressed.'

Instead of complying, he pushed her back against the pillows, anger strong in his voice.

'What the hell are you playing at? You wanted me just now and you enjoyed it. After all, there was scarcely any reason for you to fake such an ardent response to me in those last few minutes, was there?'

'You crude lecher! You disgust me,' she hissed as she tried to pull free.

'That's scarcely any way to talk to a man whose bed you're going to occupy for the rest of your life.'

She stared at him. The tone of his voice as much as his words made her skin tingle with alarm.

'What are you talking about?' she demanded fiercely.

'I'm talking about our marriage,' Zack ground back.

'You think... I'm going to marry you?' she began, almost speechless with disbelief. 'After... after this?'

'You're marrying no one else,' he told her curtly.

'You try and stop me,' she flared. 'I'll be damned if I'll ever marry you now. I hate you. You're detestable. You're nothing but a sex-crazed animal...'

'In that, we seem to match rather nicely,' Zack interrupted with soft mockery as his fingers stroked the side of her breast. 'Whatever your feelings for Greg, I can't imagine you lighting up for him the same way.'

'Damn you!' she gasped as his thumb ran over her hardening nipple, making a perceptible shiver go through her.

She hit out at him, her palm connecting with his shoulder, and, as he let her go, she slithered out of bed, wrenching the sheet after her as she tried to hide herself from his eyes. Her mouth was dry and her hands were shaking. There was an element of nightmarish unreality about the whole scene, she frantically gripping the sheet while Zack lay propped on an elbow, watching her with cynical amusement, his naked male body imbued with all the power and potency of a Rodin sculpture.

She couldn't credit the response he had drawn from her. His fierce passion had shattered completely her notions about her own sexuality, making her discover such wild, tempestuous desires in herself that she couldn't attempt to match them with the other facets of her personality.

'Get out of here,' she said in an anguished whisper as she turned away and clutched the sheet more tightly around her. 'I can't talk to you like this. I want to get dressed.'

She heard him get out of bed and then the rustle of clothing. She assumed he was complying with her demand and she did not glance round. But the next moment, still magnificently naked, he was turning her towards him. He caught hold of her left hand, and before she guessed his intention he was slipping her engagement ring back on her finger.

She made to snatch her hand away, but the blue intensity of his gaze stopped her from doing anything so rash. Her heart was thudding. In every inch of her she was aware of his closeness and his nakedness, his gaunt, autocratic features, the strong column of his throat with its rope-like tendons and the hard plane of his chest. Caught in the pull of his sexual magnetism, her hand began to tremble in his before the tremor spread throughout her body.

'No,' she protested almost soundlessly as she saw his gaze travel to her lips.

Zack ignored her, pulling her close, his kiss gentle and sensuous, as if he was tasting her for the first time. Then it deepened and she shuddered. She tried to break free, but as she turned her head away, he caught hold of her with insolent strength, and she realised too late that the sheet had slipped down to reveal her breasts.

'You look very seductive,' he said, his eyes travelling over her deliberately before they mockingly met hers. 'I've half a mind to pull you into bed again, but after the way you've just given yourself to me, I think you might be too tired to enjoy it.'

He released her and, unable to move away because of the swathe of double sheet around her legs, she sat down numbly on the edge of the bed. And, because there was something almost comic in her entangled imprisonment, she felt even closer to the brink of anguished tears. She kept her head averted while Zack, heedless of the distress he was causing her, leisurely gathered up his clothes.

'When you're dressed, I'll take you home,' he said evenly.

She felt too dazed and stunned to think. Her hands shook as after he had left the room she mechanically pulled on her blouse. The bedclothes were in complete disorder, the sheet tangled on the floor where she had dropped it, but she made no attempt to straighten the covers.

It took almost more courage than she had to join him with a semblance of poise in the sitting-room. He was standing staring out at the weir, his white shirt emphasising the breadth of his shoulders and the play of light making his face seem more implacable, the lines more attractive. She felt so shattered and empty, she was staggered at the way her heart contracted as she looked at him. Surely after this she couldn't still love him? The banked tide of pain that rose in her heart answered the question for her even as she denied it.

He turned round and she said, taking the ring off her finger, her voice remarkably steady, 'This is yours. I don't want it.'

'You really don't understand, do you?' he said, coming towards her. 'I'm marrying you, Eve. You're mine, and your involvement with Greg doesn't alter that.'

'I was never yours, never, not even on board *Rebel Lady*,' she answered furiously, her eyes smarting. 'And now I wouldn't marry you if you *crawled* from here to Cookham Bridge on your knees and begged me to, I loathe you so much. So here, take your ring, because I never want to see you again.'

He pushed the ring firmly back on her finger.

'You've made it very clear what the last few weeks were all about for you,' he said curtly. 'Well, now maybe it's time I spelled out a few details about my side of this.

We've already announced our engagement, and you're not going to make me look a fool by breaking it and marrying another man. You picked the wrong person to play games with, Eve.'

'Try not to feel too used, Zack,' she said, emotion adding an edge to her sarcasm. 'After all, our affair had its moments while it lasted.'

For an instant she saw such fury in his eyes that it frightened her. But the next second his anger was firmly in check.

'I mean to marry you,' he said. 'Your consent is frankly immaterial.'

'It's very much material,' she said, an ominous fear surfacing at the resolve she heard in his voice. 'I have to say the words, "I do", remember?'

'You'll say them,' Zack said dismissively. 'You'll say them and, what's more, willingly, because if you don't I'll withdraw in one fell swoop the entire amount I've invested in Hallam's Boatyard. I don't think I need point out the consequences of that.'

For an instant she could only look up at him with horrified eyes, and then she stammered, her voice scarcely sounding like her own, 'You ... you planned all of this, didn't you?'

He caught hold of her by the arm, his voice menacingly even.

'I rarely set out to break anyone, but when I do, I do it thoroughly. You thwart me on this and I'll not only bankrupt your father's business, but I'll take pleasure in watching the crash.'

'You're not human,' she breathed.

'But you are,' he fired back. 'The boatyard is your father's life. I don't think you'll want to see him destroyed by having it sold up.'

She stared at him and then her chin went up.

'It's an empty threat,' she said with ragged defiance. 'Even if you do withdraw your investment, we'll keep the yard going. We were managing before.'

'I'd say you'll keep going for about a month.'

It was too late now to wish she hadn't been so foolish as to taunt him by saying she'd intended all along to marry Greg. Maybe it wouldn't have made any difference even if she hadn't. His obsession for revenge went too deep. All that mattered was that Greg wanted to marry her and Zack was determined he never would. She was his woman as he had said, and his lovemaking this afternoon had been his way of reasserting his ownership of her.

In a voice racked with bitterness, she said, 'I wish to God I'd never met you.'

'You'll marry me within the month,' Zack answered, unmoved by her vehemence.

'You've already got a hold over me with the business,' she flared. 'So what's the rush?' It wasn't in her nature to plead, but in sudden desperation she changed tactics and implored, 'Look, please, can't you just forget Greg and everything that's happened?'

'I find it very hard to forget him.' She didn't answer and he went on, 'You're mine, Eve, which means your engagement to him is off. Once you've told him that, I don't expect you ever to see him again.'

It was an order, and again she didn't answer. She was fighting against an upsurge of choking tears so that even to draw breath hurt, and she had far too much pride to have the final humiliation of weeping in front of him. It seemed small consolation now that she had succeeded so ably in hiding from him the true reason why she'd said she wouldn't marry him.

She needed no further proof now of what Greg had told her this afternoon. Zack had confirmed it all. It didn't matter to him one iota that she shrank from the idea of being his wife. All that mattered to him was evening his score with Greg.

'Do I take it that your stubborn silence means I have your reluctant agreement?' Zack taunted.

'As you've just pointed out,' she retorted with a flash of husky retaliation, 'you don't need even my grudging agreement. Well, all right, if you want an empty shell of a marriage you can have one. But I swear I'll hate you for ever, and what's more, if ever I get the chance, I'll pay you back for this.'

Zack caught hold of her wrist. He had gripped her very firmly when he'd forced her into his car, and now, involuntarily, she flinched. Frowning, he pushed the cuff of her blouse up, whatever he had been about to say checked. 'I didn't realise I'd bruised you.'

'Do you really care?'

'Now you listen,' he said, taking hold of her by the shoulders, his voice low and driving. 'You can spit defiance at me all you like when we're alone, but for public consumption we're the perfect couple. Do you understand? I don't take kindly to being made a fool of, so in front of my sister on Saturday evening you're going to act as if you're in love with me. You'll do it in front of your father, too, if you have any sense. I doubt very much that he'd like the idea of his daughter marrying to save him from the ignominy of bankruptcy. So, while I'll tolerate your temper now, by Saturday, I expect you to have calmed down enough to have the act back in place. After all, you did it so convincingly before. With two days' grace, I'm sure you can manage it again.'

His voice bit with sarcasm and, retaliating, she answered, 'I'll manage. I'll manage for my father's sake, but don't you dare so much as lay a hand on me or I won't guarantee that the act won't crumble in front of everyone. You touch me or kiss me and I'll slap your face, no matter who's present.'

'You do, and you'll pay for it when we're alone.'

There was something in his voice that meant she didn't dare contradict him. Mockery came into his eyes. Grazing her cheek with his finger he taunted softly, 'Not that I mind your flashes of temper. They make you such a wild little gypsy in bed.'

He smiled cynically as he saw her blush with anger. She turned away, maddened by his sense of humour, hating him beyond measure, and yet still linked to him sexually with an inevitability she couldn't begin to explain.

CHAPTER NINE

ZACK drove her home, an icy silence between them.

'I'll call for you at six o'clock on Saturday,' he said curtly as he drew up outside her house.

She flashed him a look of pure hatred and didn't deign to reply. Instead she got out of the car in one quick movement and swept up the path, feeling the stab of his gaze between her shoulder-blades. Her skin prickled with an awareness of danger and she sped inside, thankful that he hadn't come after her.

Safe at last, she leaned weakly against the front door. With an odd mixture of relief and aching loneliness she heard the Jaguar pull away. For a moment she stayed there, her shoulders sagging, the image of angry poise she had so carefully conveyed shattering now with utter exhaustion. Wearily she went into the drawing-room and sank into an armchair.

The clock striking roused her, making her realise how long she had sat there, dazed. Getting up, she began to pace about the room, replaying the scene with Zack at his flat and filled with a furious animosity towards him. She had been so certain of his love! The thought was another knife-thrust at her heart. Suddenly she wanted to scream at fate, that had led her to be twice betrayed by love.

Zack had her trapped, and her whole instinct was to fight to get free. He might succeed in forcing her into marriage, but she'd show him she was no tame plaything, that it would be a stormy possession and scant victory.

Yet all the time, behind her defiance, was a deep sense of vulnerability. She didn't think she could endure the torment of being Zack's wife, knowing that it was Jocelyn he loved. When she fetched her father home from hospital the next morning she was almost tempted to confess to him that she wanted to break off the engagement. She knew unquestionably that he would put her happiness first, whatever the cost to the boatyard. Yet still something held her back.

Robin returned from his holiday that evening, looking very fit and tanned. In the post that was waiting for him was the written confirmation of his examination grades. Frank was obviously pleased and quietly proud of his son's success, and Eve knew suddenly that there was no way out for her. Whatever her feelings, she would have to marry Zack. He had baited the trap well, she thought with a renewed rush of bitterness. Her father and Robin meant far too much to her to see the boatyard bankrupted, to see her father ruined and the future Robin was working for destroyed.

She began to dread Saturday. In no mood for her own thoughts, which centred constantly on Zack, she worked at the yard until five. Normally when her father was at the yard she finished at midday on Saturday. But it wasn't work which meant she wasn't ready for Zack when he called for her. It was her determination to be as mutinous as possible, overlaid with an apprehensive reluctance to be alone with him again.

Half an hour after he had arrived, she finally went downstairs in a stylish blouson-top dress and bronze sandals with very slim heels. Her long, dark hair was loose and her green eyes skilfully shadowed with smoky colour. She looked deceptively self-contained, her attractiveness laced with cool provocation. In reality she was one mass of apprehension.

In the drawing-room Zack was talking to her father.

'I'm sorry I've kept you waiting,' she began, her eyes, not her tone, conveying that her lateness was deliberate.

The look of sharp attentiveness Zack gave her told her he had interpreted her remark correctly. He let his masculine gaze run over her before saying, 'You're worth waiting for.'

It was curious how only two remarks could have immediately upped the level of static. Their oblique sparring made Eve more certain of herself. When she was fencing with him it was easier to be convinced of how much she hated him.

'I didn't get away from the boatyard till five,' she said. 'You know how important the business is to me.'

The casual statement was redolent with hidden meaning. Zack lifted his brows with faint mocking derision. They were all set now for confrontation, and the knowledge gave her an odd sense of satisfaction. She couldn't make Zack love her, but at least she knew how to get under his skin.

Frank, unaware of the undercurrents, said with affectionate teasing, 'Now, Eve, Zack won't want you working in the business if you're going to put it first.'

Zack stood up, slipping an arm round her waist as he said easily, 'Eve won't want to work for long after we're married, anyway. We're both keen to start a family.'

His arm dared her to try and move away. She knew he was goading her deliberately. She coloured with a mixture of suppressed anger and embarrassment as Frank laughed and said, 'It's about time I had some grandchildren.'

She was seething with her inability to flash back at Zack, and her temper was heightened by the thought of how much having his child had once meant to her. Once again hurt fuelled her fury, and the moment they were alone together in his car she flung at him, 'You may as well know, I don't appreciate your cheap cracks. I'd sooner kill myself than carry any child of yours.'

Zack's hand tightened on the steering wheel, the knuckles white, while the other froze for an instant on the ignition key. A nerve jumped in his cheek and she felt a hot stab of triumph. For once she'd managed to strike back at him effectively, to convey how completely she loathed and despised him.

He started the Jaguar with an angry roar.

'Don't worry,' he said, his voice clipped as they pulled away. 'I've no intention of pushing you to suicide.'

The atmosphere crackled with danger. For a while there was an incalculable silence that was emphasised by the purring of the car engine. Eve clenched her hands together in her lap with the growing premonition that she'd gone too far. Finally, unable to stand the mounting tension, she announced abruptly, 'There's something else I want to get clear too.'

'And what's that?' Zack asked sarcastically.

'I'm not sleeping with you again—not ever.'

Her statement sounded far bolder than she felt.

'You mean you won't consummate our marriage?' Zack's mockery had a savage edge.

'That's exactly what I mean,' she flared. 'Our marriage is going to be on paper only.'

'You mean you want to stay true to Greg,' Zack taunted derisively, 'while being married to me?'

'If you want to put it that way.'

'I don't want to put it any way at all.' His voice cracked like a whip. 'I'm asking you for an explanation. Your reluctance to sleep with me is, after all, somewhat hard to comprehend, considering how incredible you were in bed a couple of days ago.'

She felt herself blush hotly.

'You forced me into making love with you.'

'Like hell I did! Maybe at first I was rather more demanding than you're used to, but did I force you to wrap yourself against me, to slide your fingers through my hair and make those gasping little moans...?'

'You'll never know how utterly I detest you!' she cut across him, scorched with fury and shame.

'And yet you want me,' he said, stabbing her a hard glance. 'Odd, isn't it, the attraction we have for one another?'

'Want you?' she said, her voice contemptuous and far from steady. 'Walking the street would be preferable to sleeping with you again!'

This time she knew she'd gone too far. Zack stopped the car, and in a defensive panic she edged away from him and stormed, 'I don't love you, so don't you touch me.'

'You didn't seem the moral idealist when you were playing me off against Greg,' he ground out, snatching hold of her arm.

'Leave Greg out of this!'

'When you make him central to the whole issue?' Zack's fingers tightened as he sneered. 'What is it you find so appealing about him, Eve: his integrity, his steadfastness...?'

'He's worth ten of you!'

'Small wonder you got ripped off by your fiancé. You don't know the first thing when it comes to men.'

'I wish I'd never told you about Simon,' she said wildly as she hit out at him.

Zack grabbed hold of both her wrists and, hating his superior strength, she gasped, 'I wish I'd never told you the first thing about me!'

Her stormy eyes clashed with his before sexual awareness flashed its invisible sparks between them. Suddenly her heart was racing, not with anger but with the knowledge that it was inevitable that he should kiss her. She heard him swear in a savage undertone, as though he was bound by the same magnetism that held her captive. He tilted her chin almost angrily, his mouth coming down to claim hers.

The instant shock of response that went through her filled her with despair. Why was it that not even her loathing lent her any immunity to him? It was the last coherent thought to surface in the instant before his lips parted hers. Held possessively against his strong man's body, she felt she was drowning. She had to save herself. She *would* save herself. Yet, instead of repulsing him, her fingers hesitated before sliding in an unconscious caress to his neck.

Zack raised his head, his blue eyes searching hers with a blazing intensity, while hers gazed back with something darker and more confused than resentment. Time had stopped. They seemed linked together so strongly at that moment that neither of them could break the spell. And then Zack bent his head slowly and kissed her again with a slow, sensual demand that made leaping fire run through her veins.

For an instant she fought a desperate war with her emotions as she willed herself to stay cold and passive in his arms. She felt Zack's hand travel sensuously up her spine, pressing her breasts against his broad chest. Involuntarily she gave a low, husky moan at the rocketing of feverish pleasure.

'Kiss me,' Zack breathed harshly. 'Kiss me back, Eve.'

His mouth covered hers again, tormentingly gentle and yet determined, allowing no denial. Helplessly she tangled her fingers in his hair, giving him the response he had demanded. She didn't know how long the kiss lasted, but when he finally raised his head it took a moment for her spinning world to steady.

He ran a lightly caressing finger down her face, and she caught a glimpse of triumph in his eyes as he mocked softly, 'Are you still sure you're going to want to stay out of my bed after we're married?'

She couldn't answer immediately, and then she said, with all the more hostility because she was so shaken, 'I suppose... I suppose I'm to pay the interest on the money you've lent my father.'

'Not *every* night,' he said, the glint of anger in his eyes in conflict with his tone.

He started the car again and pulled back on to the road. Eve reached for her clutch-bag from the dashboard and searched for her lipstick. After the thoroughness with which he had kissed her, she needed the reassurance of knowing she didn't look as ravished and bewildered as she felt.

It seemed that all Zack had to do was to touch her to transmute her hatred of him into a driving hunger for him. The thought filled her with panic. Guided by her compact mirror, she touched up her lipstick, conscious that her hand was far from steady. She didn't see the narrowed, sharply observant gaze Zack slanted at her.

As she fastened her bag, he asked, his voice deceptively derisive, 'Tell me, because I'm curious. Was what you told me about your fiancé being unfaithful to you the truth? Or was it a way of arousing my... protective instincts?'

The question was unexpected, but in any case she wasn't anything like calm enough to think of the wisest way of answering it.

'I'm not in the habit of telling lies,' she began stormily. 'I've never yet met a man worth loving.' She went cold as she immediately realised her error. Amending it quickly, she added, 'That is, until I met Greg.'

'You don't seem to have much luck where love's concerned, do you?' Zack mocked.

Her emotions were suddenly far too near the surface for her to risk a haughty reply. She sensed rather than saw the astute look he slanted at her.

'Did you tell your father we've set a date for our wedding?' he asked after a slight pause.

'Yes,' she answered tightly.

There was another short silence, and then Zack commented, 'There are some cassettes in the glove compartment. Find something you like and put one on, will you?'

She did as he asked, thankful for the unaccountable respite he had given her to gain mastery over her chaotic emotions. Strangely, after such a turbulent beginning, for the rest of the journey Zack didn't put any real pressure on her again. It didn't stop them fencing, but there was nothing barbed in Zack's faintly mocking comments, and against her will she found herself remembering the time they had spent together when she had believed in both him and their relationship.

The roads were quiet and the countryside hazy after a day of brilliant sunshine. Meadowsweet and tangled clumps of dog-roses grew along the hedgerow. Now that she was less emotional, she could guess why Zack had let up on her. He didn't want his sister to sense how electric the atmosphere was between them.

As they neared Oxford he confirmed her suspicions by commenting with a trace of dry humour, 'Just remember, my little gypsy, that we're supposed to be the perfect couple. So try not to spoil the illusion in front of Suzanne.'

'I haven't tried acting farce before,' she snapped caustically.

'Well, I'll be watching today's performance closely, so it had better be good.'

He turned into the broad circular drive of a double-fronted house built of honey-coloured stone. As he brought the Jaguar to a halt, she caught his gaze, and the tacit warning he gave her that she had better not ignore what he'd said. Certain that in another minute she'd ruin the performance even before the curtain went up, she got out of the car, defiance in every line of her slim body.

Zack's sister and her husband James welcomed her with genuine warmth. It was hard to believe that what had every appearance of being a happy, informal family occasion was in reality nothing more than a charade. A familiar angry hurt started to tug at her. She took her usual steps in dealing with it. Zack wanted a convincing act. Well, he was going to get one. Except that she was going to play her part so superlatively that she would underline for him with every word and gesture the complete hypocrisy of her performance.

Each time she spoke to him she put a soft caress into her voice. She lingered dreamily on everything he said, her eyes holding his. The glint she saw in his gaze told her that he was both needled and amused. It pleased her. Now he could see how little he really knew or understood her, despite the completeness with which she had given herself to him physically.

Though she must have taken him by surprise, he reacted as smoothly as though her misty adoration was an everyday occurrence. It was only as they went into the dining-room that he drew her to him, kissed her lightly and murmured sardonically, 'Don't overdo it, darling.'

'You haven't seen anything yet,' she whispered sweetly.

The conversation round the dinner-table was lively and outwardly relaxed. Zack's two little nieces, Carleen and Gemma, were full of excited questions about the wedding. Eve, who had wanted to take a hearty dislike to Zack's sister and family, found it impossible. She felt a bond with them already, despite everything. She didn't want to think how different everything would have been if Zack had really loved her. It hurt too much.

She had already drunk more wine with her meal than she did usually, but she let James top up her glass again. She needed something to stiffen her spirit so she could get through the rest of the evening.

As soon as the dinner was over the two little girls asked if they could go out and play in the garden.

'For a little while,' Suzanne agreed. 'Until it's time for bed.'

Absently Eve reached out, turning the flower arrangement that made the centrepiece of the table so that she could admire it. She noted the dusky pink carnations. Their fragrance had haunted her throughout the meal. Somehow carnations seemed to have been the leitmotif of her relationship with Zack. Brightly she announced, 'A love of flowers obviously runs in the family. Do you know Zack sent me a bouquet every single day before we got engaged? My whole office was filled with flowers.'

Zack's hand closed firmly over hers, the force of steel behind the caress as he said, 'You bring out the romantic in me, sweetheart.'

'Let's have coffee,' Suzanne smiled. 'Shall we drink it in the living-room?'

'Eve takes hers black,' Zack said casually.

He knew perfectly well she didn't, but he evidently felt she needed sobering up before her waywardness outran her discretion. The thought that he was probably right did not improve her mood. She gave him a quick look of resentment before volunteering, 'I'll help you clear away, Suzanne.'

In the kitchen Zack's sister switched on the percolator while Eve set out the cups. They chatted for a while before Suzanne said impulsively, 'I can't tell you how happy it makes me to see you and Zack together. You're so obviously right for each other, and he's been through such a lot.'

'You mean with Jocelyn dying the way she did,' Eve said, her voice tautly expressionless.

Suzanne drew a deep breath and said quietly, 'That was just the culmination. It must have been hell for him that last year. I don't know how he stood it. And then Jocelyn started that doomed affair... And, well, you know what happened after that.'

Yes, Eve did know. But Zack's devastation over his wife's death didn't give him the right to ruin *her* life, to take his revenge on Greg through her.

'It was rough on him,' was all she managed.

'It was more than just rough,' Suzanne said softly, her eyes remote as she focused on memories that were still painful. 'I thought Jocelyn would destroy him.'

They were interrupted by Gemma, Suzanne's six-year-old, who burst into the kitchen, sobbing indignantly.

'Carleen says I've broken her doll... and... and I didn't!'

'There, ssh,' Suzanne began as she bent to comfort the little girl. 'Now, what's all this about?'

Eve turned away, her thoughts in turmoil. She went into the hall. Through the open door to the living-room she could glimpse Carleen, who was sitting on Zack's knee, held against the crook of his arm while he examined her doll. There was a sudden ache under Eve's ribs, and she felt she couldn't endure it.

Desperately she tried to push Suzanne's words from her mind. After all, she thought angrily, what had changed? Suzanne had only confirmed what she knew already: that for Zack there would only ever be one woman, his dead wife.

'You've mended it!' Carleen squeaked delightedly as Zack handed the doll back to her.

She slithered off his knee as Eve entered the room. Zack glanced up, and inadvertently she caught his gaze. It wasn't the moment to think of how much she had once wanted them to have a family of their own, not if her outward composure wasn't going to break completely.

She wondered if Zack sensed what an ordeal the evening was turning into, because despite the easy conversation and laughter they didn't stay too late. Her head ached with the strain of pretending. She sat next to Zack on the sofa, contributing to the talking less and less.

When she leaned forward to put her cup down on the coffee table he stretched his arm casually along the sofa, so that when she leaned back it was to find her shoulders were against his sleeve. Unobtrusively, she straightened up, but Zack's hand dropped firmly to cup her shoulder. As he carried on talking to James, his hand caressed her gently. Resentment gnawed at her. Zack was too dominant and powerful, too adept at outmanoeuvring her at every turn. Yet behind her anger an aching pleasure stirred at his touch, making her heart contract. Why couldn't Zack have loved her? In the firmness of his personality and the strength of his physique, she seemed to have discovered an answer for every need in her nature.

She hadn't even realised she had relaxed against him when he commented humorously, 'We'd better be making a move. You're getting so comfortable, sweetheart, that you'll be asleep in a minute.'

He stood up and helped her to her feet. Marshalling her energy, she managed to smile and maintain the act to the last. As they drove away, Zack remarked, 'I'd no idea you were so good with children. You made quite a hit with Carleen and Gemma over dinner.'

'And with your sister, too,' Eve replied mutinously. 'I hope you were satisfied?'

Her answer seemed to amuse him in a wry sort of way and, instead of picking her up on it, he said with more tolerance than she had expected, 'Well, we seem to have our wedding plans more or less sorted out, apart from our honeymoon. Where would you like to go?'

Running through her mind like a refrain were the words Suzanne had said. 'I thought Jocelyn would destroy him.' Abruptly she said, her voice sharpened with sarcasm, 'As we met on the river, why don't we continue the romance on water and hold hands in a gondola? How about Venice?'

'We'll be doing more than holding hands wherever we go, but if Venice appeals to you, we'll have a fortnight in Italy.'

'I can't be away for a fortnight.'

'And why is that?' Zack asked. 'Does the thought of a fortnight alone with me frighten you?'

'Wouldn't you like to think it?' she flashed back.

His taunt was too near the truth. Once they were married, how long would it be before she had to face up to the fact that, despite everything, she loved Zack to the point of desperation? The sudden admission of the stark truth shocked her like a blow, and she gave a slight gasp of dismay.

Zack glanced at her, and then said with a curtness that she knew spelt danger, 'Are you going to go on being so defensive, or shall we for once try a more adult approach and get this sorted out?'

'Get what sorted out?' she asked with the last remnants of rebellion.

'Don't push me, Eve. You have a highly amusing repertoire, but right now you've provoked me enough. You know exactly what I mean. You owe me some explanations, and I'm not taking you home till I've got them.'

His implacability should have sparked her to renewed hostility, but it didn't. Their sparring had lost its appeal.

She loved him too unbearably to go on playing the shrew. In that moment she knew that, whatever the consequences, she couldn't marry him. The ache of incompleteness of life without him would be infinitely preferable to the constant torment of being married to him, knowing he would never love her.

She bit her lip. Her heart was hammering with apprehension as she tried to steel herself to tell him. His love for Jocelyn was an obsession, but surely she could plead with him to let her go and not to bankrupt the boatyard. She'd called him inhuman. But he wasn't. He could be remarkably kind and understanding. She tugged a handkerchief out from her sleeve, making Zack flick a hard glance at her.

'Are you crying?'

'No, of course I'm not,' she said in a muffled voice. 'Why should I be?'

'Why, indeed?'

His remark was cryptic, but she felt too defeated to ask him what he meant. As they approached Windsor, Zack said, his tone telling her that whatever her objections the topic wasn't up for debate, 'Let's stop off for a drink. We're going to talk this out on neutral territory.'

She guessed he meant territory where things couldn't get as violently out of hand as they had the other evening at his flat. Ahead was a hotel, its white gables picked out in coloured lights. Zack turned the Jaguar into the car park, drew to a halt and then tilted her chin up. In the dimness of the car interior she couldn't read his expression clearly; the bemused tenderness she had thought she had glimpsed fleetingly in his eyes had to be her imagination.

'I haven't been crying,' she insisted stubbornly.

His comment confirmed that she must have been mistaken an instant ago, for there was nothing the least bit tender in his voice.

'Stop being so damned mutinous, before you exhaust my patience.'

With his hand at her elbow he escorted her into the hotel. His touch was no more than firm, but she felt like a prisoner being escorted under guard.

The hotel bar, with its dark beams, exposed brickwork and low-key lighting, had a relaxed atmosphere. In the background, music was playing softly. Zack steered her to a table that was tucked away in an alcove, and then went to the bar to fetch their drinks.

Eve huddled into the corner of the banquette, nerving herself for what she had to say. As Zack put her glass down on the place mat in front of her, he commented drily, 'Try not to look as if I beat you the moment I get you home.'

She raised her eyes to his, swallowed nervously and then said in a cramped voice, 'Zack... I... I'm not going to marry you.'

He sat perfectly still, his eyes fixed on her. The gaunt lines of his face were accentuated by the muted lighting which heightened the strength of character that could be read in it. Then he drew his brows together, almost quizzically, and said, 'Of course you're going to marry me, my little elf.'

'Don't call me that,' she flared, strength coming back with anger. 'Don't you ever use another meaningless endearment to me again, because I'm *not* going to marry you. You're wasting your time playing the hypocrite, because I know perfectly well why you want me...'

Her voice broke without warning and he interrupted tersely, 'Do you? Then maybe you'd enlighten me.'

'I'm not going to marry you so you can get your revenge on Greg,' she said on a rising note.

'*What?*' he demanded.

'And whether you've got a hold over me or not, I won't marry you,' she swept on. 'I'm not going to live with you knowing all the time that you still love Jocelyn. I'm not going to wait until you think you're even with Greg and then don't want me any more. So if you're hell-bent on revenge, you'll just have to bankrupt the boatyard, because...'

'What the hell are you talking about?' Zack erupted, reaching out to catch hold of her hand.

She snatched it away as if his touch burned her. A tear ran down her cheek and she brushed it away.

'And I picked this place so we'd keep things calm!' Zack said with the hard anger of a much-taxed man.

'You needn't worry,' she snapped, her voice emotional and unsteady as she glared at him. 'I'm not going to embarrass you. I'm the sort that hates scenes, remember?'

'The night I met you isn't something I'm likely to forget.'

He caught hold of her wrist to emphasise what he was about to say.

'Let go of me,' she protested, a shaky catch of breath betraying finally how close she was to a flood of anguished tears. 'I want to go and neaten myself up.'

Zack's relentless blue eyes searched her face. Then he relented.

'All right,' he agreed. 'And then we'll finish this somewhere else.'

She stood up and walked away from him, trying to keep her slim shoulders squared. She was crossing the foyer on her way to the ladies' cloakroom when she saw Robin in the entrance of the restaurant, chatting with a group of friends. Suddenly she wasn't seeking a temporary escape from Zack and the chance to pull herself together. She was intent on total, desperate flight.

She went quickly up to Robin and touched his sleeve. He glanced round and then began in surprise, 'Hi, Eve. What are you doing here?'

'Zack and I stopped off for a drink. Robin, have you got your car?'

'Yes, why?'

'I need it. Can you get one of your friends to give you a lift home?'

Robin took hold of her arm and moved away from the noisy group he was with so they could talk more easily.

'What on earth do you want my car for?'

'Look, I haven't got time to play twenty questions with you,' she said, urgency making her impatient. 'I've had a row with Zack and I want your car so I can get away from him.'

'Aren't you being a bit hasty?' Robin asked. He threw out his hands in mock capitulation as he saw the stormy light come into her eyes and said tolerantly, 'Yes, all right, you can have my keys. But Zack's only going to...'

'Thanks,' she said gratefully, taking the keys and not stopping to hear the rest.

CHAPTER TEN

SHE raced across the car park, jumped in Robin's old Fiat and pulled away, fighting down the sobs that, if she allowed them to, would wrench her apart. Shakily she wondered how long it would be before Zack realised she had gone. A little further on and it occurred to her to wonder what his reaction would be. Well, she didn't care, she thought fiercely. All that mattered was that she was free from him.

She had the vague nagging comprehension that somehow escape from a man like Zack wasn't going to be as simple as a cut and run. Now she realised what Robin had started to tell her and which she in her frantic haste hadn't stopped to listen to. Zack was very likely to follow her home. Her father was having dinner with friends, and she knew he wouldn't be back till late. Without him there for protection, there was no way she was going to risk a second confrontation with Zack, not till she rallied a little. She desperately needed some time to bring her emotions under control, and the only safe refuge she could think of was the boatyard.

It was all in darkness as she drove in, the sheds inky shadows and the river a gleaming expanse of onyx where the white cruisers stirred eerily with the slight current. Lights from the bank opposite sent golden shivers dancing over the blackened water. She got out of the car and walked slowly towards the jetty. She was in a state of numb stillness that she didn't want to fade, because when it did she would have to face the unbearable pain of being less than whole.

She stepped on board one of the cruisers and sat down in the stern, finding a measure of calm in the faint whisper of the river and trying to avoid thought. She was still sitting there, her chin cupped in her hands, when there was the sound of a car. Startled, she glanced up to see the twin circular headlamps of a Jaguar turn in through the boatyard gates.

In sudden panic she got to her feet. She had to get off the boat before Zack found her. She clambered along the narrow side of the cruiser. And then she gave a startled cry as in her high-heeled sandals she slipped. There was no chance to save herself and, arms outflung, she fell into the river with a silence-shattering splash.

She came to the surface, gasping for air, shocked by the coldness of the water. Striking out for the jetty, she saw Zack, jacket removed, drop to his haunches and stretch an arm towards her. He grabbed hold of her, hauling her bodily out of the water. She was dripping wet, her dress clinging tightly to her, her hair streaming.

'You stupid little fool!' Zack shouted at her furiously.

Standing in front of him, soaked to the skin with both sandals lost, did nothing for her dignity. Still breathing hard she shouted back, 'I suppose you thought I'd flung myself in the river because of you!'

'No, thank God, you've got more sense. Not much, but more than that.'

'Don't you insult my intelligence,' she exploded.

'I'm starting to wonder if you've got any,' he fired back with equal heat.

She was about to reply angrily when her vision swirled. Did Zack really look so grim-faced with concern? She swayed slightly and immediately his arm went round her.

'God, don't cap it all by fainting on me,' he said.

'I'm not going to faint,' she said weakly, pushing a feebly protesting hand against him. 'And what's more, I'm not going to stay here and be shouted at.'

Zack swung her into his arms as though she weighed no more than a child.

'Agreed,' he said tersely. 'I'll shout at you at my place.'

He strode with her in his arms towards his Jaguar. Setting her on her feet, he opened the passenger-door for her.

'I can't get in,' she protested irritably. 'I'll drip water all over your car.'

'After this evening, do you think something as trivial as that is going to bother me?' he asked with what sounded like exasperated amusement as he pushed her inside.

He got in alongside her and she darted a glance at his profile. For some reason he wasn't anything like as angry with her as she might have expected. Yet it wasn't possible that there was tender humour in his dark eyes as, sensing her eyes on him, he slanted a look at her. Her heart started to beat faster with wild, crazy hope.

In a rather small voice that seemed to have lost its resentment, she said, 'How did you know I'd be here?'

'Because when there's something troubling you, you seem to need to be near water.'

'Why did you come after me?' she began before continuing in a rush, 'Because it's no good Zack. I meant what I said, it's over between us.'

'That bastard of a fiancé of yours really did a good job on you, didn't he?' Zack said with curbed harshness. 'I suppose it's because of him that you can't trust me.'

'I don't see I have very much reason to trust you,' she said, starting to shiver. 'Not when you're trying to force me into marriage and threatening to bankrupt the yard.'

'I've no intention of bankrupting your father,' Zack said, cutting across her.

'But... but you said...' she began accusingly.

'You don't have to remind me,' he said caustically.

She looked at him with puzzled eyes. She was too emotionally exhausted to begin to make any sense of what he'd just said. Was he telling her he was letting her go without a fight or... She didn't dare complete the thought. Foolish hopes could only lead to more painful disillusionment.

Despite the fact that she was barefoot, she didn't want Zack to carry her into his flat. It made her feel too defenceless. He saved the energy of arguing with her by picking her up and not setting her on her feet until they were inside.

'Quite the mermaid,' he remarked, a rakish gleam in his eyes as he looked at her.

She realised that, with her pale dress clinging to her, none of her curves were hidden from his appreciative gaze. Blushing, she said coldly, 'What can you lend me to put on?'

'I'll find you a shirt while you have a hot shower to warm up,' he told her.

The steaming water of the shower soon stopped her shivering. She let the jets stream over her skin, basking in the warmth. Stepping out, she was draping a towel around her when Zack came in.

'Here, put this on,' he began.

'Not with you watching me,' she retaliated. 'And you might have knocked.'

She felt hopelessly flustered. Slipping on one of his shirts could only heighten her femininity. It made her unreasonably angry with him.

'For heaven's sake,' he said, 'I have seen you naked before.'

He snatched the towel from her and pulled the shirt round her. With her face flaming, she thrust her arms into the sleeves and was still fumbling with the buttons as he caught hold of her hand and led her into his bedroom.

Realising suddenly what he was doing, she resisted and said with fierce alarm, 'You let go of me!'

Zack pushed her down on to the bed.

'Shut up and listen, because you and I are going to talk.'

'Talk! I would have thought we'd said everything there was to be said.'

'All we seem to have done since Thursday is to say a whole lot of things neither of us meant.'

'You speak for yourself!' she retorted. 'I meant everything I said to you.'

Amusement tugged for an instant at Zack's mouth.

'Especially the fact that you don't want to marry me,' he supplied for her, putting a finger on her lips before an answer would spring there.

A quiver ran down her spine. Her eyes, dark and wary, met his. If only he knew it, she was completely vulnerable. In the last few minutes he seemed to have robbed her of every defence.

'There's quite a lot I think you have to tell me,' he said evenly. 'But first I want to talk to you about Jocelyn.'

'I don't want to hear about Jocelyn,' Eve whispered tightly. 'I know enough about her already.'

'Just listen,' Zack insisted grimly. 'I'm not letting you walk away until you've got straight whatever upside-down facts you seem to have accumulated.'

For once she didn't contradict him. There was a slight pause and then he said, as though long reticence made the words difficult, 'Jocelyn and I were married for three years. She'd been a model and she was something really special. It wasn't just that she was stunningly beautiful. She had a sort of brittle charm that fascinated people.'

Eve dug her nails into her palm. Why did Zack have to torture her like this? He was making her scream inwardly with jealousy by talking about the woman he loved.

'What I didn't know,' he went on soberly, 'was that her high-strung charm was going to take her over the edge. We'd been married no more than a few months when she had a nervous breakdown. Her doctor said she'd got to stop living at such a fast pace. I felt partly responsible, and so as much as I could after that I tried to keep her away from the pressures of being a company chairman's wife.'

He paused again. Eve's gaze went to his face, noting with a compassion that wiped out her own hurt the sharp lights of pain in his eyes.

'Only it turned out Jocelyn couldn't slow down. She needed life in the fast lane, the adulation she was used to in the modelling world. And, once the first infatuation was over, there wasn't enough between us to replace the excitement. With plenty of time on her hands, she started to look for ways to prove that she was as beautiful and desirable as when she was at the height of her modelling career.'

'You mean she... she had other men?' Eve asked falteringly.

'She craved a man's attention the way addicts are driven for a fix,' Zack said wearily. 'I wondered at first if it was some kind of reaction because she'd lost the baby, but I don't think so. The baby hadn't been planned, and she was furious when she discovered she was pregnant, so furious that I never expected...' His voice expressionless he said, 'That was the first time she tried to kill herself, after she miscarried.'

Instinctively Eve reached out to cover his hand with hers. Huskily she said, aching so much for him, she found it hard to speak, 'Oh, Zack, I'm so sorry.'

He nodded, taking her hand in his and giving it a gentle squeeze. In all their moments of closeness there had been nothing quite like the tacit communication of this instant. Zack drew her against him and continued, 'Jocelyn had psychiatric treatment for several months after that. I hardly dared let her out of my sight for a time in case she tried suicide again. It was just after she'd been in for another short spell of hospitalisation that she met Greg. He was working for me at the time. I was very taken up with the business or I'd have realised what was going on sooner. I warned Greg to stay away from my wife because the last thing she needed was another love-affair. When he didn't, I fired him. Only, I was too late. I came back earlier than I'd originally intended from a business convention to find she was gone. Greg had persuaded her to go away for the weekend with him. Apparently they had a violent argument. He must have realised at last how unstable she was and he walked out on her. Jocelyn phoned me from the hotel in Cheltenham where they'd been staying and sobbed out the whole story. She was full of remorse and I wasn't in the mood to be very understanding, I told her I'd drive and pick her up.'

'And on the way back,' Eve whispered, guessing the rest, 'that's when the accident happened.'

Zack shot her a quick glance and then said, 'So you don't know. No, there was no accident. Jocelyn killed herself.'

There was an aghast silence. Eve eased away from him, her shocked eyes on his face, her hands gripping his arms.

'You mean...?' she stammered.

'Jocelyn was already dead when I got there. The door to her room was unlocked and she was lying on the bed. There was an empty bottle of whisky on the carpet, and in her hand was the bottle of tablets. She'd taken the lot.' He frowned, and Eve, helpless to conceal her horror could herself see the scene that his thoughts must be conjuring up.

'Even now,' he said quietly, 'I don't know if she really intended to kill herself or if she hoped I'd get there in time to stop her. She'd left a note. It had just one word. "Sorry." There was an inquest, but because there was no conclusive evidence the coroner generously brought in a verdict of accidental death. Jocelyn had always been careless with tablets. He said it was possible she'd been confused by drinking and hadn't meant to take an overdose. Even the note was ambiguous.' Heavily, Zack added, 'I'd have liked to have believed him, only I couldn't. That note tormented me because I knew it was a helpless apology for taking the final way out. The apology was for me, but she'd killed herself over Greg.'

It took a moment for Eve to gain control over her voice enough to whisper thickly, 'Zack, I'm sorry. I'm sorry, too, for all the awful things I've said. When I said about... Forgive me, I just didn't know.'

'I should have told you about it,' he said quietly, his eyes meeting hers, a sad smile in their depths. 'I almost did, soon after we got engaged.'

'I know,' she said with a flash of comprehension. 'It was when I mentioned the piano at your house.'

Zack brushed her temple with his lips, drawing her back into his arms again.

'Then maybe you'll understand, too, why I didn't,' he said. 'The last thing I wanted was to revive the past. I'd been over it too often, asking myself again and again what I should have done to prevent the tragedy.'

'But it wasn't your fault,' Eve said. 'Greg was the one who walked out on Jocelyn, not you.'

'Yes, but I was her husband.'

The simple sentence explained it all to her. Suddenly she saw Suzanne's comment in a different light. Zack might have realised his marriage to Jocelyn had been a mistake, but he couldn't divorce her. If he had, he would have judged himself no different from his father who deserted his mother because she'd been disfigured. However ill Jocelyn had become mentally, he would have stood by her.

And, instead of believing in him, she'd listened to Greg. She was torn with self-reproach. She'd taken the facts available and construed them in the worst possible way so that they supported what Greg had said. She was shaken by the knowledge of how much she had wronged Zack. Unable to find the words to express how she felt, she told him instead with her body. Murmuring his name in a racked whisper, she slid her arms round his neck.

With a faint groan Zack enfolded her tightly in his arms. Eve clung to him a moment. Then she raised her head, his eyes full of tenderness meeting his, before Zack kissed her with a hunger as though of years and years of deprivation. She arched her neck, her heart beating with fierce exultation as Zack's lips at last left hers to trace kisses down her throat. Despite the fool she had been, somehow, miraculously, he loved her. She felt his hand cup the soft weight of her breast, and she gave a faint gasp, glorying in the fact that beneath the thin shirt she was naked.

'Eve,' he muttered as he opened her shirt. 'Oh, God, what am I doing? I want to get everything straightened out between us, not make love to you.'

She lay back against the pillows, lifting her arms and inviting him to lean into her embrace. Running her hands lovingly over his back and shoulders, she whispered, 'Things *are* straight between us. I love you. I've always loved you.'

Zack kissed her deeply, and then with a mammoth effort of will he raised his head. She felt the tremor of restraint in his arms as he pulled back from her.

'No,' he said, 'there's something else we've got to get clear. I want you, Eve, you know I do. The reason I made love to you so fiercely the other evening was because I was so furiously jealous. All I could think of was proving the attraction between us was stronger than...'

'I never loved Greg,' she said, interrupting him. 'He told me you were marrying me for revenge, to get even with him over Jocelyn. I was so desperately hurt and so determined you'd never know how much I love you, I flung that lie at you that I'd broken our engagement so I could marry him.'

'So that's what happened! I've been so angry with you the last couple of days that I couldn't work it out. It was only today, when you kissed me in the car, that I realised that, whatever you'd said, you loved me, and that I was going to get the truth out of you even if I had to put you across my knee to do it.'

'You wouldn't have!' she said with an indignant laugh.

He gave her an attractively amused smile and said, 'You're my woman, Eve. I wasn't going to let you go easily. Not when there could never be anyone for me but you.'

'Not even Stephanie?' Eve said, confident enough now to tease him again.

'Stephanie,' he repeated with a touch of wry humour. 'She was another complication in all this.'

'What do you mean?'

'There was nothing of any deep significance between us, but until I met you we had been seeing a lot of each other. After Jocelyn's death, the company became my life more and more. Stephanie had just split up from her husband, which meant that she had no objections to working long hours when the need arose, and if there was any social function I had to go to she usually came along. But our relationship always stopped short of bed, even when one evening she made it very plain she was available and willing. It was just after I'd first met you, and I couldn't get you out of my mind. Far from wanting

Stephanie in bed, what I wanted that evening was you. So as not to hurt her pride, I told her I hadn't slept with anyone since Jocelyn's death. She took it that I was too tied to Jocelyn's memory to get involved seriously with another woman, and I let it go at that. That's what I thought she must have repeated to you at my office that day. It was the only explanation I could think of for why you'd handed back my ring.'

Eve turned and ran her hand sensuously over his chest, savouring the hard-muscled feel of him.

'I should have trusted you. But when I looked back, everything seemed to have happened so quickly between us that I couldn't believe you'd really fallen in love with me so quickly.'

'Neither could I,' Zack said humorously as he moved to press her back against the pillows. 'When I saw you sitting on the steps by the river that evening... I can't explain it. I felt as if you'd been there waiting for me after I'd spent a lifetime searching. It was almost a jolt of recognition, something I'd never encountered with anyone before, as though we'd known each other before in some other time and were finally united again.'

'I felt it too,' she admitted, happiness filling her.

'When you told me you were involved with Greg Neville I told myself that I'd been wrong, that it had to have been some trick of the twilight that had drawn us together. And then you gave me that look of provocation from across the room.'

'I didn't mean to.'

'Whether you did nor not, I knew after that I intended to have you. You're in my blood, Eve, a part of me. You're all the things I thought I'd lost and forgotten.'

She reached up and touched his face, tenderly tracing the attractive line that grooved his cheek.

'Oh, Zack, I love you,' she whispered.

'Then don't you ever do a damn-fool trick like running away from me again,' he growled.

'I won't,' she promised. 'How could I, when I belong to you?'

The shared memory immediately flashed between them as their eyes met. She had once told him defiantly that she'd always be beyond his reach. His answer had been that he'd tease her about that defiant statement one night when they made love. She coloured slightly, but her eyes laughed with his. She knew now that his tender humour was part of his loving her. Now it was back to unite them, making them complete again.

The thought made desire kindle within her with a sudden fierceness. She saw the darkness of passion in Zack's eyes, and when he bent his head and kissed her she responded with an abandoned ardour, ripples of fire racing through her body.

Tempered by his mounting hunger, she could sense the strong, swift current of his deep love for her. She shivered with pleasure as his knowing hands caressed her.

'I'd better get you under the covers before you get cold, my love,' he said huskily.

Her heart raced with a mixture of excitement and delight as she felt him tense against her loving touch.

'I'm sure you'll think of a way to keep me warm,' she murmured, a hint of answering laughter in her voice.

Zack slipped the shirt from her shoulders before sliding his palms the whole length of her back as he held the slight arc of her against him. Exultantly she gave herself up to the enchantment of his lovemaking, her body welcoming his as it had welcomed no other.

And then, as she tumbled with him through the waterfall of desire, there was only the maelstrom of sensation, and beyond that the mutual rapture and peace of true fulfilment.

 **Harlequin Romance**

Coming Next Month

#3001   UNCONDITIONAL LOVE   Claudia Jameson
Coralie's new life in Salisbury is disturbed when Jake Samuels and
his son arrive and Jake offers her a decorating commission. Coralie
knows she can handle the arrogant Jake, but she's convinced
something's wrong in the Samuels household.

#3002   SEND IN THE CLOWN   Patricia Knoll
Kathryn, as her alter ego Katydid the Clown, had been adored by
thousands. But as Reid Darwin's temporary personal assistant life is
no circus. What did she have to do to win even a word of praise
from her toughest critic?

#3003   BITTERSWEET PURSUIT   Margaret Mayo
Charley isn't looking for romance—she just wants to find
her father. Yet thrown into constant contact with explorer
Braden Quest, who clearly opposes her presence on the jungle
expedition in Peru, Charley is aware of the intense feelings sparking
between them....

#3004   PARADISE FOR TWO   Betty Neels
Prudence doesn't regret giving up her own plans to accompany
her godmother to Holland. She finds her surroundings and her
hostess charming. However, she can't understand why the arrogant
Dr. Haso ter Brons Huizinga dislikes her—and tells herself she
doesn't care!

#3005   CROCODILE CREEK   Valerie Parv
Keri knows returning to the Champion cattle station can mean
trouble—yet her job as a ranger for Crocodile Task Force requires it.
Meeting Ben Champion again is a risk she must take—but it proves
more than she'd bargained for!

#3006   STILL TEMPTATION   Angela Wells
Verona is happy to accompany her young friend Katrina home to
Crete, but her excitement is dampened by Katrina's domineering
brother, Andreas, who expected a middle-aged chaperone, not an
attractive young woman. Suddenly Verona's anticipated holiday
turns into a battle of wills....

**Available in September wherever paperback books are sold,
or through Harlequin Reader Service:**

In the U.S.
901 Fuhrmann Blvd.
P.O. Box 1397
Buffalo, N.Y. 14240-1397

In Canada
P.O. Box 603
Fort Erie, Ontario
L2A 5X3

Gull Cottage

The sun, the surf, the sand...

One relaxing month by the sea was all Zoe, Diana and Gracie ever expected from their four-week stay at Gull Cottage, the luxurious East Hampton mansion. They never thought that what they found at the beach would change their lives forever.

Join Zoe, Diana and Gracie for the summer of their lives. Don't miss the GULL COTTAGE trilogy in Harlequin American Romance: #301 CHARMED CIRCLE by Robin Francis (July 1989); #305 MOTHER KNOWS BEST by Barbara Bretton (August 1989); and #309 SAVING GRACE by Anne McAllister (September 1989).

GULL COTTAGE—because one month can be the start of forever...

Harlequin Regency Romance™

Romance the way it was *always* meant to be!

The time is 1811, when a Regent Prince rules the empire. The place is London, the glittering capital where rakish dukes and dazzling debutantes scheme and flirt in a dangerously exciting game. Where marriage is the passport to wealth and power, yet every girl hopes secretly for love....

Welcome to Harlequin Regency Romance where reading is an adventure and romance is *not* just a thing of the past! Two delightful books a month.

Available wherever Harlequin Books are sold.

REG-1R